BEHIND THE MASK

A.J.Morris

Authorbynature

To "Ninja Norman" the fly catcher of the YHLP writing group without whom this story would never have started; and to Kayleigh Evans, founder of the YHLP writing group who's tireless enthusiasm keeps us all going.

PROLOGUE

The Earth rumbles and shakes and then is still.

Vibrations that begin in the planet's core rise upwards until they reach the peaks of the mountains which burst open, spewing out fiery rivers of steaming lava. After the first blinding brilliance of light there is only a grey gloom that seeps into corners, seeking out shadows until they merge and become one.

Flames begin to dance on the branches of ruined trees, fires that will burn until their hosts are charred echoes of their former selves.

Only one thing moves in the heavy silent air.

Through the gloom, through the clouds of dust and smoke a black vehicle, dark as the night and twice as vast halts where the city once stood.

Slowly its doors glide open.

CHAPTER 1

The photo hangs on the wall, browning with age. Her, her mother, and brother; two children standing on a sandy shore with the waves rolling endlessly behind them. It is a faint, blurry reminder of a time gone by. A time so long ago that it is a distant memory. The time when life was normal; when they had lived and laughed and played in the sun. When they had been a family, a family with a home. A home with green grass on the lawn, flowers in the borders and blue wooden shutters to keep out the heat of the sun. A home where their mother had prepared meals, and they had all sat around the long wooden table that filled the kitchen and talked and laughed.

Before. Before it all began.

Before the war to end all wars, the war that turned the sky orange and the earth black.

Before they came.

They had come in their thousands; clad head to foot in black, faces covered with metallic helmets, bodies covered in leather. Robots with beating hearts and empty souls; driven by the one thing that united them, to control.

They had swept through the land like the locusts that swarm over the pages of the bible. Killing at random, obliterating all traces of freedom and happiness. The men had fought, as men do when their homeland is threatened; when peace and comfort become so important to them that they cannot bear the thought of losing it. But lose they did; they couldn't stand against the metal-faced men with robot souls. The women had run, hidden, and taken shelter in the darkest recesses of their homes. She had come here, to this village in the mountains where she had watched from afar as the city burned.

They hadn't come after them, the men in leather, something they didn't understand until now.

They needed them. They needed the women so that they could continue. They needed their bodies as vessels to create more soulless humans with dark hearts. So that the control would continue and spread until the whole planet was covered in them.

The men, those that remained, were enslaved, working in factories to make more metal helmets, more weapons, more leather clothes: or to labour on farms to feed the armies and the cowering terrified women. Not that much of the food was spared for the women. Here in the hills, in their sanctuary, they had begun to grow their own food in sheltered spots hidden away, patches of reluctant soil filled with vegetables and fruit. This was her task now. To tend the land, bake, and make her contribution to this village of women. The women left behind to serve, or to grow until they themselves were ripe to be harvested like fruit on a vine.

Somewhere out there in this land that was just beginning to become green and reclaim the planet's surface, as land does when given time, was her brother. He had been too young to be of any threat to the men when the war came so he had been taken, as all young boys had been, to the "camp." Perhaps he was working in one of the factories alongside the beaten broken men. Worse, maybe, he now wore a metal mask of his own.

She had no idea what had become of him, but she would find him. She had promised, the day she had seen him dragged screaming from their home while she hid like a coward in the cellar. She would find him.

"Clara?" A woman's voice sounds at her door. "It's me, Elle. Let me in."

Clara opens the door and lets in the nearest thing she now has to a family.

Elle is tall and thin and has long tattered hair that would be blonde if it weren't stained brown with dirt. It tangles and knots and falls from her grimy headscarf to her waist. A waist around which she has knotted her brown skirt to stop it falling onto her worn sandals. Elle, like Clara, has lived fifteen years in this village, eking out an existence from the land and feeding the community. Elle, like Clara, has now lived on this planet for twenty-five years.

Fifteen years of being afraid.

Fifteen years of trying to be safe and stay hidden from the metal-faced men.

Until now.

"They have found us." Elle's voice is a whisper.

"They always knew we were here." Clara shakes her head, her hair a red mane of curls that despite the dust and grease still bounces and has a life of its own. "They just didn't need us."

"They are saying they are coming." Elle's voice trembles, and she clings to the wooden chair in front of her to prevent herself from falling. "They say they need more women for the breeding houses."

"I should think they do." Clara shrugs. "Women can only breed until a certain age if they survive the breeding itself to get there."

"Aren't you scared?" Elle's long-fingered hand, scarred and worn with work clutches at Clara's sleeve.

"Of course, I am." Clara embraces her friend. "But until the time comes, we cannot think about it. They will not take us all and there are younger and sweeter than us in this village."

"They say," Elle's voice breaks, "that they are metal *down there* also."

Clara laughs.

"Where on Earth did you hear that silly? Of course, they aren't. If they were, they would have no need of us. They may be a different race of men to those we once knew, but they are still men underneath it all."

Elle freezes, her hand tightening on Clara's arm.

"Listen!"

There is no hiding the sound that approaches. Vehicles, many of them, climbing the hill to the village.

"They are coming."

The men enter the village in convoy, a line of vehicles with containers at their rear to take the women to the breeding houses. They have their orders. Some must be left where they are; the older and the infirm to live out their lives in this meagre existence, toiling to provide the food that is taken every week into the city, and the very youngest so that they may grow and fulfil other needs. These women left behind also take in the laundry that cannot be dealt with by the workers in the city or get taken to scour and scrub in the houses of the officers. Any girls born in the breeding houses are raised, if healthy and able, to also work in the background of the machinery that is this army or to support those already in its service.

Those that aren't live a short life.

There are enough women in these outposts still for the menial tasks; and only the best specimens go to work for the officers and the governors.

The men know that the very finest of the women are kept for the officer's private use, housing them in lavish rooms wearing silks and lace and bathing them daily to keep them clean and sweet smelling. The men are only used to those in the breeding houses. Fed enough to keep them alive and washed before each breeding so that they do not offend the men. They have no names, no meaning. They serve a purpose. For pleasure, the men go to the houses in the city where the best of those that can no longer breed are kept for the men's use when they have time for recreation.

The men do not question this. It is how they live. It is how it has always been since the great invasion. The mothers and sisters they once knew are vague memories and have no impact on their lives now. So, they raid the villages picking and choosing the ripest of the apples allowing the rest to fall. Women have no part in their life. They are here to control, to improve, and to spread the law of the government further across this planet.

Germin is young, he has yet to meet his twenty-first year. He remembers little before the days when he did not hide behind his metal face. Sometimes a vague memory tugs at him; smells, sounds, something warm and comforting that wraps around him and makes him feel safe. But it is distant and does not affect him. He just knows his routine and follows it. His first journey to one of these villages had brought those memories flooding back. The smells of cooking, of women, the sound of dogs barking in the dirt. That had been hard and had tugged at something lost deep inside, but now he is unmoved as he watches the women and girls dragged from the houses and lined up in front of them.

The officer walks the line, opening their mouths and checking their teeth, walking around them to study their physique. Once or twice, he lifts their skirts and thrusts his hand underneath.

The women cower and some cry out, but none dare to move. He pulls them into place, those to go, those to stay. Germin spots a woman with bouncing red hair and something in him stirs. He hopes that this one will get taken back to the city as he is now of age to enter the breeding houses. The puppets in the pleasure house suit a purpose but he has yet to find one that excites him. This one would. He imagines her red hair bouncing as he bends her over in front of him and heat rushes to his loins.

"You!" The officer raises his hand to him and disturbs his reverie. "Take these, vehicle one, and get ready to leave."

Germin walks forward and raises his gun at the bunch of tattered cowering women in front of him.

"Move. In. Now!" The metal helmet makes his voice sound robotic, and he can see the fear in their eyes.

As he closes the door on the vehicle he looks back. The officer is at the red-haired girl, his hand darts between her skirt and she snatches herself away. Germin feels something twisting in him, something that feels like anger. He should have been able to do that, to feel what lay beneath her dirty skirt. In his head, she was already his.

The officer has pulled her forward; she is to come to the breeding houses.

Behind his metal face, Germin smiles. His chance will come when it comes to the picking, he will choose her; hopefully, his seed will impregnate her, and he will sire a great soldier.

But it is the act that he knows must happen before a child can be born that fills his mind. Germin has never felt lust before; it is not something he has understood.

Until now.

CHAPTER 2

Elle stares out of the window as the vehicle jolts downhill. Beside her is a little girl who is crying in terror.

"It's okay my sweet." Clara strokes the girl's hair. "You are young, too young, there will be jobs for you in the kitchens, I'm sure."

Clara's eyes meet Elle's, and she registers the same fear in her friend.

"It's okay." She reaches out and takes her hand. "We are still together. That's all that matters."

"What if they separate us?"

"They won't," Clara smiles. "We will be together, I'm sure."

Inside, she is not as sure as she makes herself sound. She has no idea of what will happen to them, but they must keep calm; hysteria could have fatal consequences.

"Keep your head down," she tells the young girl. "Stay by me, hold my hand and we will be fine."

The vehicle is drawing close to the city. Gone are the grey ruins, the windowless towers, the facades with hollow empty eyes that were left after the great war. Slowly the city is beginning to grow. There are new buildings, tall and dark against the sky. A sky that is never blue now; it is smoky brown, and when the pale sun tries to come through it glows orange. Despite it all, even with the trepidation of what is to come, Clara is fascinated as the city looms larger. Vehicles move on newly laid roads. White house's surround squares with fountains; fountains of clean water sparkling in the pale light. There are flowers too, and she can see women working; emptying rubbish into bins, carrying objects back and forth between the houses. The black-clad men are everywhere, walking in lines or driving the grey square vehicles. But there are no children. In all of the gardens, where the earth is trying to repair itself, there is not one child.

The buildings are taller now and she sees great glass elevators climbing the outside of them. A long white structure with four towers comes into view, a row of steeply climbing steps leading towards it. This is where they stop. Flags fly in front of the building and there is an emblem above the huge arch at the entrance.

"Out."

The door swings open and one by one the women stagger out. The young girl is clinging to Clara, shaking in fear.

"You." A soldier points at her. "You go there."

He gestures to a door where another figure clad in black is waiting.

The girl starts to cry, clinging to Clara, her body shaking.

"It's okay," Clara whispers. "Just go, please. Go, be safe, please."

With her heart wrenching Clara pries the girl's hands off her arms and pushes her away. The girl's eyes look up, pleading, begging for her help.

"Go." The soldier steps forward.

"You have to GO!" Clara shouts. "Don't you understand, you have to do what they say!"

"No." Hysteria is gripping the young girl, and she spins away. "No, no, no!"

Ducking under Clara's outstretched hand she begins to run.

Clara's cries are silenced by the sharp crack of the gun.

Blood seeps on the ground spreading over the pale stone. More soldiers move forward and lift the girl's lifeless body. Beside her, Clara hears Elle sob.

"Watch." Says the soldier. "This is what we do to those who disobey."

Clara stares at him, trying to see through the metal face. Are those eyes that she can see? There is the glint of something moving deep inside. Clara doesn't hold with the tales that these men are part metal and part human; these are just men. She can smell their sweat inside the black leather. Hear their breathing. But they are men who have been changed beyond all recognition.

The soldier returns her stare. This one could be trouble. He takes in the tangled dirty hair and the small breasts beneath the tatty garments. Her legs were long, he can see that much. Her eyes, glaring at him, are pale green. She will clean up well. Maybe he would select this one for himself. Such spirit would work well in a soldier's child.

"That way." He points towards a door on the other side of the courtyard. "That side for processing."

The queue of tear-stained women makes its way to the door. Inside is a long corridor, dimly lit, that leads to a giant hallway. Smells of fragrant soap fill the air. There are women here. Women in black uniforms with hair shorn close to their heads. One by one they take the arrivals from the queue and into rooms where, side by side, they are stripped and scrubbed. Their bodies are shaved of hair, everywhere, and the hair on their heads is washed and roughly brushed. Some have their hair cut short, so it sits in spikes around their faces, but both Elle and Clara are spared this final indecency, their locks are left long and ragged, wet against their skin. They are each given a loose shapeless garment of rough grey cloth and hard sandals which hurt their feet.

Standing in line as they move towards another

door Clara looks back at Elle and sees her long hair, dark and wet against her face. Elle tries to smile at her, but her attention is caught by the sounds behind the door.

"They are screaming." She gasps. Why are they screaming?"

"I don't know." Clara shakes her head ignoring the sickness in her own stomach.

In a few short minutes, she knows all too well the cause of the screams that fill the air; as the branding iron presses hot and painful into her flesh.

They stand in groups, huddled together for safety, arms burning and sore from the branding; a flock of grey birds, cowering, trembling, wondering what awaits them next. One of the women raises her hand and beckons them to follow her down a myriad of passageways that twist and turn until they reach a large room with a table at its centre. The centre of the table is lined with bread and cheese. The women fall on the food and eat like animals, washing the food down with a rough, coarse wine. Clara looks around as she chews on another piece of dry bread. Around this room are smaller areas each leading to doors. At the opposite end of the room to where she sits there is a grand carved door with gleaming polished handles. Instinct tells her that this leads to where the men are. After they eat, they are taken to the smaller rooms and pushed inside. Ten women in each room. There are beds made with rough blankets and pillows; bowls of water stand in the corners. In the room where Clara finds herself two women already sit; beyond the last of the beds are iron bars; beyond the bars more beds where more women lay.

"Animals in a cage." She hisses. "Is this what we are to them?"

"Ssh!" A woman with cropped dark hair points at a camera in the ceiling. "They hear everything."

Beside her Clara feels Elle start to tremble.

"Come on." She takes her friend's hand. "Sit."

Taking the bed next to the shorn-haired woman and placing Elle alongside her, Clara looks around the room. At least there are windows which allow some air to flow through and let in enough light to set the dust particles swirling.

"I'm Marie," the woman offers. "You are?"

"Clara. This is Elle."

"Welcome." Marie gives a half smile. "If that is the word?"

"Indeed." Clara scowled.

"You have beautiful hair." Marie reaches out and touches the curls which are drying in the warmth of the room. "You will attract attention, that's for sure."

"Is that a good thing?" Clara glares at her.

"Maybe." Marie smiles. "If an officer takes a

fancy to you, you will live in a beautiful apartment and wear beautiful clothes."

"Like a slave." Clara scowls.

"Yes, but a slave who is well fed and housed and who only has to serve the needs of one master. For those who stay here, well, the masters are many."

"How does it work?" Clara, despite wanting to deny that she is in this hell hole, feels that she needs to prepare herself for what is to come.

"This isn't a whore house." Marie lays a hand on her leg. "They don't come here for pleasure, they come here to breed. The doctors will test you and only when you are in that part of your cycle where you are able to conceive will you be put forward. Then if you are chosen you stay with that man until the time is past. Then you wait for another test. If you are with child, you move to another part of the building; if you are not, you come back here to wait another month."

"What do you mean stay with that man?" Elle leans forward to listen.

"In the breeding rooms. They will come to you many times when their work is over and attempt to create a child."

"Is anyone else in these breeding rooms?" Elle is shuddering.

"No," Marie half laughs. "They are small, little more than the size of the bed. The men do not like performing in front of others. Some may be embarrassed."

"Embarrassed?" Clara snorts, "Why?"

"Not all men are the same. They don't want another man laughing at them."

"Why would they laugh?" Elle stares at her.

"My dear girl. In the same way that you and I are a different shape so are the men, in all parts of their bodies, some are big, and some are small. The small ones prefer to be hidden."

Marie chuckles to herself at the thought.

"Have you," Elle swallows hard, "have you been there, in the breeding rooms?"

"Me?" Marie chuckles again. "Of course. I am getting older, the time will come when I will be in the laundry rooms, or worse. But for now, I am still of breeding age, so I stay here. I don't get picked so often now, there are prettier morsels on offer, but I have had three successful breeding's, and two that failed to survive. The last few times I have been chosen no child has settled in my womb, so I think my time here is coming to an end."

Elle is astounded that Marie can talk about the subject in such a carefree manner. But Clara can see that it is a shield, a way of surviving what has happened and what is still to happen to the woman beside her.

"What were they?" She asks softly.

"Boys." Marie nods. "The ones that lived. The two that didn't were mercifully girls. They never got to know life before it was taken from them."

Clara leans back on the wall behind the bed and closes her eyes. She does not doubt that with her mane of red curls, she will attract attention and be chosen. How will it feel she wonders, growing big in the belly and unable to move. Unthinking she runs her hands over her stomach and as she does so can feel a familiar ache begin. A half smile flickers on her face. There will be no visit to the breeding houses for her yet.

The days are long and roll endlessly into one another. They rise when the clock chimes early, eat a meagre breakfast, and watch as the men take those assessed to be prime for breeding. The officer with the medical kit comes every week, takes blood, and records the results. Clara rests easy those first few weeks. The day after they had been brought here the blood had stained her garments and she was taken to be cleaned, they knew that there would be no need to test her for the coming weeks. Elle is not so lucky. Clara watches as the officer comes to their room and consults the machine in his hand. He points to Elle and gestures at her to follow him. Clara stares at Elle in horror; watching her friend looking back over her shoulder as she is led away.

Four days pass until Clara sees Elle again. When she returns, she is different. Her head hangs and she shrugs her body into herself, arms over her stomach. There are marks on her neck and chest.

For a long time, she will not speak. Then when she does the tears start to fall.

"Oh Clara," she sobs, "what will happen if I am with child?"

"Well, I suppose you will have it." Clara moves onto her friend's bed and places an arm around her shoulders. "Was it as bad as you feared?"

She felt Elle shudder and then collapse against her.

"I hated it, I never want to do it again. We are just pieces of meat to them. He came in and threw me on the bed and then forced himself into me. Three times in one night. Then again in the day. Sometimes he made me stand against the wall; once he laid me over the chair and stood behind me. It hurt and I cried out, but he wouldn't stop. The final day he only visited the room once. But that was the worst. I started to back away from him, I was sore and torn and I didn't want it anymore, so he hit me, again and again."

Clara wraps her arms around her friend and holds her tight. Marie, sitting silent in the background gets up and walks over.

"The best way my dear child is to simply accept. Relax your mind and let them do it. Close your eyes and wish it to be over quickly. They never stay long; they play their games with the women in the pleasure houses. Where I, no doubt, will be moved soon if they deem me good enough. For the third month now, I have not bled. My breeding days are done but I feel at my age I will be condemned to a life in the sweatbox that is the laundry. Still, that will be preferable. Only the cruel visit the older women in the pleasure houses."

"The pleasure houses?" Elle shudders. "Pleasure?"

"Some would call it that," Marie smiles softly, "but fear not, that is many moons away for you. You are young, if you are not with child this time then it will be three weeks before they take you again."

"Yes." Clara stroked her friend's hair. "And I will be next."

Inside Clara feels a knot of fear; her day must be close. She has avoided selection for long enough. But she will take her turn as Elle has done and bear whatever it is they do to her.

Several rooms away Germin is taking his place in the selection line. It is his third visit, and the red-haired girl is yet to be pulled out. Perhaps she has been chosen by someone else and is already growing a child? Is she not yet ready for breeding? Perhaps today will be the day? But when he enters the room and looks down the line of downcast faces, he can see she is not there. Angry at being denied his fantasy again, Germin chooses a small dark-haired woman with wide thighs. She will do for now.

Behind the glinting metal of his mask the officer

watches Germin push the woman ahead of him into one of the small cubicles. He has a feeling that the young soldier has desires for a certain red-haired beauty who has caught his own attention. He had seen him watching her closely in the village, staying close behind her on the journey to the breeding houses. He would see about that. From the day he plunged his fingers beneath her skirt and felt her smooth silken thighs against his hand he had been waiting. In all his visits into the breeding houses or the village he had never seen a woman more beautiful. The thought of her excited him. He would use his rank and claim her first, when she appeared. He had stolen a look at the doctor's notes. Not long to wait now, her time was near, and she would take her place in the line.

CHAPTER 3

The day that Clara is selected, Elle is sick. Not once, not twice, but four times between waking and breakfast and then again after. The medic is called, and he pronounces her with child. A successful breeding. In a few months she will move into the rooms where those with child wait to produce their offspring. For now, she will stay where she is and continue to eat, sleep, and grow the child within her. Clara can feel her friend's pain as she watches her curl up on her bed. Bearing children should be a pleasure, filled with a warm glow of anticipation; but in this place it is a time of dread; filled with fear of the unknown and of what will happen afterwards.

Clara joins the line of women that snakes along the room in a ragged wave. Ten of them, all pronounced fit to breed. They have been washed afresh this morning and smell of soap and warm skin. The men in front of them all wear the uniform of black leather and metal-faced helmets. To the left of the line is one that is smaller and shorter in appearance than the others; he has slim snake-like hips, and his legs are lean, he appears young. From the moment he takes place in the line Clara can tell that his eyes, although hidden behind the expressionless mask, are fixed only on her. This makes her uneasy, she senses the intention coming from within him and knows that he will choose her; there will be no avoiding the situation today. But as he steps forward, with determination, to make his choice, the officer who has been watching over the selection also steps forward.

"Back in line." He speaks abruptly.

He turns his metal stare onto Clara.

"With me."

Clara stares at the long, leather clad arm as it points to a door to her left. Her stomach turns slightly. Does this mean she has been chosen by the officer; or does some worse fate await her? She walks on, aware of the man behind her and the stance of the small soldier who is clearly disappointed as she walks away. The officer is tall, he has broad shoulders beneath the leather suit and his thighs are strong and muscular. She suspects him to be older than the men that he leads. He directs her to a small room, barely more than a cubicle, where the essentials of her stay have been laid. A bed, a toilet, and shower so that she can keep herself clean. For this Clara is grateful, she will enjoy, whatever else happens in the time, the pleasure of the warm running water. The officer gestures to the bed.

"Undress." He tells her. "And wait."

Then he is gone, closing the door behind him.

Clara stares at the door and hears the click of the lock. Slowly, she removes her clothes and lays naked and vulnerable on the bed. It seems like an age before the lock clicks open and the officer returns into the room. He glances at her, then begins to remove his leather trousers.

Clara watches fascinated as the harsh leather peels away to reveal strong legs, coated with fine, fair hair and at their top a sight she has not seen since her brother was a child. Clara had never seen a grown man naked before. She had heard the women talking of course and had listened into many conversations since she had been in the breeding houses, but none of it had prepared her fully for what was in front of her. Yes, she knows what happens when the breeding's take place; yes, she knows that men are different, but to see it all in front of her is a shock. Something is happening to her own body; she can feel a heat coursing down her stomach to a place between her thighs. She wriggles on the bed, frustration mixing with the trepidation she feels. He starts to walk towards her with only his lower half void of clothing. The metal helmet is still on his head. With a flick of his hand, grabs her hips. She feels herself being rolled onto her face and then lifted so that she perches on her knees. Then a pain sears through her body as he plunges deep inside her. Clara snatches herself forward, screaming, and feels a hand grab at her hair.

"Keep still."

Trembling, sobbing, Clara grits her teeth and feels his body slapping hard against her, then as the tension inside her releases, he pulls away. Clara falls to her face and gasps, waiting for the pain to subside. Behind her the door clicks, and she is alone.

She curls herself tight into a ball, folding in on herself as Elle had, and waits for his return. She lays on the bed for what feels like hours until the darkness outside the one small window tells her that he will not return that day. Getting weakly to her feet she steps into the shower and allows the tepid water to wash over her. Then she pulls on the rough white garment she has been given and climbs onto the bed. There is nothing else for her to do, this is her new prison until the time is past.

Four days she is there, and he visits many times, each time it is the same until the night of the final day.

He is late in the evening, as ever, but there is something different about his demeanour as he walks through the door; he appears relaxed and as he draws closer Clara smells alcohol.

The usual routine begins, and he pulls off her garment but this time he does not turn her over; he lays her on her back and lifts her legs as he bends over her. With his metal face this close to hers

Clara can clearly see the glint of his eyes and stares at them, forcing herself to try and make contact and not shy away. She is used to the act now, she doesn't scream or try and pull herself away, it must happen so she has tried to close her eyes and will herself to relax. The more she relaxes she has discovered the easier it becomes. But this feels different, he is looking at her; his eyes fixed on hers as he began the usual rhythmic thrust against her. Unthinking she raises her arms and wraps them around his shoulders; something is building inside her, something she doesn't understand but it is something to be welcomed and encouraged. She finds herself clinging to him, pushing up to meet him and all the time staring into the faint mirror of his eyes until at the final moment she gasps and flings her head back, eyes closed, her body shuddering. For a moment, when it is finished, he stays where he is, his metal head collapsed on her neck. Then, his eyes still fixed on her, he gets back to his feet.

Clara is confused; she doesn't want him to move from her, or to go, to leave, she wants him to stay. She sits up and feels an overwhelming sadness as she watches him dress. In all the time he has been here has never once spoken to her.

"Will you come again?" She fears the answer in whatever form it will come.

"No." His voice is deep. "We have completed the time."

Clara hangs her head, a drooping flower with red petals. The sadness that covers her is overwhelming and totally unexpected.

When she lifts her head, he is gone.

As he walks along the corridor Aleric feels something that he has never known before. He has visited the breeding rooms many times and sired many children in his five and thirty years. But he has never felt like this. Maybe once or twice when he was young and filled with infatuation, the women he served had taken over his fantasies. But since he had visited the pleasure houses, that had stopped. There were women there whom he visited regularly, who knew his name and looked forward to his visits. He spoke to them; they understood they were forbidden to disclose anything that went on. Unlike some of his peers Aleric was not a cruel man; he never indulged in some of the tortures that other men got sexual pleasure from. But as an officer he never allowed emotion to come in the way of his work. Women were to be used, for pleasure, or for breeding, nothing more. But this one was different. The way she had looked at him, clung to him. He dreaded the thought of her being with child and not being able to visit her for nine months. For the first time, he prays that a child had not been made and that in four weeks' time he can bring the red-haired girl back to the breeding rooms.

In the four days that Clara has been away Elle has been sick, constantly. She is pale and anxious and shakes whenever the metal-faced men enter the room. She cannot understand Clara's melancholy when she returns.

"Are you not glad it is over?" she whispers. "If there is a child you will not have to be chosen again until the child is weaned."

Clara looks at her; she cannot explain what she does not understand herself. Every day she looks up as an officer comes to the door to call those due for selection, but it is never him. Somehow, despite the androgynous appearance of the uniform they wear she knows that it is not him. He is different, taller, stronger, he has a presence that fills the room when he enters. Then the day comes when the doctor takes her away to a small room and examines her. She hesitates; what does she want from this? To be with child and face the unknown, the pain of childbirth but nine months of safety; or to not carry a child and go back to be selected again?

If she could be selected by only him, she would go for selection every time, but she hears the tales the other women tell when they return sobbing, tales of cruelty and abuse. What if when her time to be chosen comes and he is not there?

The doctor looks at her curiously. Then writes notes in his computer.

"Successful," he tells her. "But I have orders to give you this."

Before she can pull away, he plunges a needle deep into her arm.

"Take these." He holds two tablets. "Today. The bleeding will start sometime tomorrow, and the child will be gone."

"Why?" Clara stares at him.

But he does not answer, just gets up and opens the door.

As she leaves the room, she does not see the tall dark figure of Aleric watching as she is led away.

Elle is incredulous.

"They did what? Why? What does this mean?" Then as a thought strikes her. "We will be separated; in a few months I must go to the birthing rooms. You will be left here."

"Ha." Marie is listening. "If she is not with child by then she will have been moved anyway. I have heard of such things before. Perhaps the child would be weak or deformed but it is too early to see, that is what I don't understand."

"He told me he had orders." Clara is already beginning to feel the muscles of her stomach tightening.

"Orders?" Marie nods. "This I have heard of also; someone has taken a shine to you and your pretty red hair and wants to visit you again."

"No!" Elle is horrified. "Not so soon!"

"Every month." Marie shakes her head. "Until she is with child, or they decide she is of no use and move her to service. Although with her face and hair the pleasure houses will be in line for her. They like to have a selection of pretty meat, not just the faces of those that can no longer produce a child. Unless whoever has taken a liking to her wants her for themself."

"An officer?" Elle stares at her friend. "That would mean leaving here forever, living in a place with food and fine clothes."

"And never having a child." Marie looks at her. "Those who are chosen to live with the officers are sterilised. They will never give birth."

"Why?" Clara looks at her, puzzled.

"It is just the way it is. The men must all have equal chance to sire a child. The women who live in the fine houses stay only until their looks fade and then they are culled."

"Culled?" Clara feels fear creep up her spine.

"Officers and generals have many secrets. Firstly, they will remove their metal heads, so the women see who they really are, secondly, they talk when they are drunk. The women know all, and it cannot find other ears."

Try as she might Clara cannot comfort Elle. The thought of being separated from her friend sends her declining into a deep dark spiral that worsens as she watches Clara lying in her bed clutching her stomach and willing the pain to pass.

Germin has been watching the lists; he knows that the red-haired girl's pregnancy has been terminated, he can see the medical note on her record when he scans the list of women to be put forward for selection; what he does not know, is why? She has become an obsession; every day he scans the lists and when she is not available leaves with what to him is a poor substitute. Having her is all he can focus on, he knows until it happens, he will find no satisfaction. What he does know is that she will be back in the lines soon and this time, he, Germin, will claim her. Aleric is away gathering more women; he will miss this selection. This is Germin's chance to see the red hair tumbling in front of him.

Clara sees him as soon as she stands in line; she remembers his slightness and the way he stands. She sees his metal head turn and follow her as she walks into the room. There was no sign of the officer who had taken her before. Clara felt her heart sink; she had hoped that he would claim her again, that this was why she had been given the termination. But he was not there, and as one by one, the women were taken away, her hope faded.

Germin feels heat pouring through his body as he sees Clara standing in the line and as he points to her, his hand is shaking. At last, there is no

Aleric to prevent him claiming the prize.

"You." The officer with the clipboard points to Clara. "Go."

Down the corridor she walks, and into another small basic room that will be her home for the coming days. Wave after wave of disappointment wash over her as she accepts that the officer who she had held and clung to, was not going to be with her. This time it is different; this time he watches as she undresses; this time he barely removes his lower garments before he throws her against the wall, crushing her with his weight, his metal helmet hard against the back of her skull. Clara's nails scrape the wall as she tries to stay upright and then she is thrown face down onto the floor as he kneels behind her. When it is over there is blood in her mouth and on her knees. She retches slightly as he stands behind her. Not moving, lying perfectly still, she waits until he is gone before she staggers to her feet and is violently sick.

There is no pleasure in the days that follow; not turning to cling to the broad shoulders of a man who gazes intently at her as she lies beneath him. No words are spoken. There is just the act, as violent as it is short and always quickly completed. No heat courses through her loins this time. Then the fourth day comes, and she hears the door open. She braces herself and turns on her knees knowing the routine by now. As sure as the sun rises weakly in the orange sky, he grabs her legs roughly and begins to punish her with his body; punish her for being a woman, for being the one who will hold his seed and make him a father of soldiers. At the end as he pulls away, she turns on her side and can see him as he reaches for the leather trousers; his skin pale and dotted with freckles, a down of hair as red as her own descending from his stomach. On his right thigh is a mark, a vivid purple scar from some long-ago wound.

A wound that she herself had cleaned and held fast with stitches. Clara starts to breathe hard and heavy, sickness rising within her.

As Germin heads for the door a word reaches his ears that makes his blood run cold.

"Brother."

CHAPTER 4

Elle watches her friend return from the breeding house and sees instantly that something is deeply wrong.

"What is it?" She clutches at her hand. "What did they do to you?"

Clara's face is bedded with a sorrow deeper than any Elle has ever seen.

"Germin." Clara sits on the bed shuddering violently.

"What? Germin? Is he here? Have you seen him? Is he safe?"

Clara raises eyes filled with such pain that Elle knows without question what has happened.

"Clara." She whispers. "How do you know?"

"I saw his scar." Clara is gritting her teeth against the bile in her throat.

"He didn't recognise you?"

"How would he? He was but a child and we were all so young. His memory of me will have long faded."

"But the child you will bear." Elle whispers. "You must tell someone. Surely the child cannot live?"

"I hope there will be no child." Clara's voice is breaking. "I must speak to the women and find a way of making sure it never comes."

"You must tell them. The men." Elle insists. "Even they must understand."

"And do what? If I can't be selected, by any soldier, they won't want me; what will become of me then? There must be a way, someone must know. Marie will know, she will help me."

Germin sits in his tiny room in the barracks and stares at the floor. Could it be possible? He has a vague memory, long since drilled into the distance of a girl who had held him and played with him; a girl who had heard him screaming as they pulled him away. Slowly he removes his metal helmet. His hair is red, and his eyes pure green. He looks at himself in the mirror and sees, for the first time, in his own reflection, the face of the woman he has just served as a bull will serve a cow looking back at him.

Aleric is angry. He storms the corridor to the selection room. He had left instructions that the red-haired girl be kept for him. But she had been called and now that little boy Germin has been with her. It makes Aleric feel sick, to think of someone else feeling the pleasure of her body. Of all the breeding's he has carried out, month after month over the years he has never wanted to go back and breed again with the same woman. But with this one he does; he had ordered the termination so that he could claim her again and once more feel her clinging to him and looking at him with her emerald eyes. Now, if she was with child, it would be many months before he saw her again, if she survived the birthing to return. To order another termination was the only option; but then to prevent this happening again he would need to claim her and take her to his rooms. He knew that this would mean almost certain death for her in a few years, but in those few years she could live a pleasant life away from the smells and fears of the breeding houses.

And she would be his.

Elle looks back with tear filled eyes as she is led away. Her belly is swelling now, and she is to be moved to a place where the food is better, and she will have sunlight to nourish the child inside her. This she is glad for, but she must leave Clara; pale, depressed Clara who sits shuddering in the corner, all her life and vivacity gone. Someone has taken the fighting bull and gelded it, it is now just another member of the herd. Her friend she had always looked up to, whom she had relied upon to see her through, no longer has any interest in the day or the night. but just sits and stares. But Elle still needs her; she can't face the rigours of birthing without her; but for the first time in fifteen years, they would be separate, unable to even speak.

A sob bursts from her and Clara looks up, starting as if from a dream at the departing figure. Something within her stirs and she runs to the gate.

"We should have hidden." She reaches for her friend's hand. "We should have hidden and not been found."

"I don't want to go." Elle is sobbing, "I want to stay with you!"

"It's okay." Clara holds her small, thin, hand. "We'll be together again soon, one way or the other."

Elle looks at her and nods. She understands. Clara is yet to know if the incestuous act with Germin has made a child. Marie is trying to find herbs that will wash it away for her; but if that doesn't work then Clara will soon be moved also. If it does work, then it will be only a matter of time before she joins Elle. Clara will not be left from the lists.

Marie is standing behind her.

"I have them." She whispers. "When you take your evening tea tonight, put them in your cup."

"Thank you." Clara nods. "How?"

"There are a few here who know the way to get such things. But we never ask. It's safer that we don't know."

Clara nodded, she understood. Staying safe was all that had mattered until now; but her life had changed, what was worse; the fear of being culled or carrying the child of your own brother?

To her tortured mind death was a better option.

Germin watches her; he hides in the shadows of the corridors and watches through the bars of the rooms the woman he now knows is the sister that had been wiped from his mind. Daily things come back to him; smells of warmth and food; laughter, mountains, and running streams of water. Tender hands soothing his wounds and comforting him. He sees her sitting still and sad in the corner of the room that serves as both bedroom and living quarters for this ragged bunch of wretches, the lustrous hair now lank and lifeless. He sees the horror in her eyes and feels it begin to echo in his own heart. He wants to go to her, to tell her he remembers and to apologise for what he has done. But that would make him weak; and he is trained not to be weak. Women were for breeding; and that is all he had done, sire the future generation. Why then was it so difficult to live with, the knowledge that he had bred with his own sister? Why did it make him want to allow the tears to fall from his eyes and his stomach to vomit? So, he watches, riddled with guilt, silent in the shadows, and sees her as she pours a handful of leaves into her tea. He doesn't know what they are for, but he can guess; he has heard the tales of the women in the pleasure houses with their remedies to prevent children for those that are not sterile. He won't say anything. This is for the best. One thing he knows for sure, however many times the red-haired girl stands in front of him he will never choose her again.

CHAPTER 5

The room is dark and silent. The women are sleeping when a scream rents the air and wakes them. They stumble, groping for light to see what is wrong. They see Clara, her white gown drenched in blood, writhing on the floor, knees bent to her stomach in pain. Marie is first to her side.

"Ssh. Ssh." She strokes her hair. "Let it pass. It will end soon."

Tears are streaming down Clara's face; terror fills her eyes. The last time had not felt like this; that had passed quietly, this was ripping the insides out of her with jagged fingers.

"Help me." She gasps. "Please."

Marie looks down at the pool of dark blood on the floor and knows something is wrong.

"Guard!" She shouts. "Guard, we need help!"

The medical officer leans over Clara and places his hand on her wrist. If this were any other woman, he would walk away and allow her to die writhing in her own blood; but this one is different. This is the one that officer Aleric wants; if he lets her die then his own departure from this life won't be far behind. He raises his hand to two soldiers at the door.

"Help me." He shouts. "Get her to my surgery."

Together they drag Clara to his sterile room, leaving a slug's trail of blood behind them. He lays her on the bed, attaches a drip to her arm and plunges a syringe into her stomach. He watches as the blood flow begins to slow. The girl is as white as the sheets she lays on. He could be too late. Her breathing is shallow and her heartbeat faint. He plunges another syringe into her arm and lines more fluid into the drip. He needs blood. But that is reserved for those who are injured in fighting, not for women. There is a footstep at the door. He knows who it will be.

"Will she live?" Aleric's voice is harsh.

"Maybe." The medic gets up. "She has lost a lot of blood. A transfusion would be best."

"Impossible." Aleric shakes his head. "You know this."

"Then we will have to wait and hope."

Aleric nods and looks at Clara. Even unconscious she is desirable.

"Sterilise her."

"What!" The medic looks aghast. "That will surely kill her in this state."

"Sterilise her and then she can have blood to recover as it is on my orders. If it works, it works. It's the only option. Sterilise her and then bring her to me."

Clara sleeps for five days. When she wakes, she sees the tubes in her arms and tries to rise, but she is strapped to the bed. A woman is in the room with her. She has never seen a woman working here before. But she is tending to Clara, changing a heavy pad of material between her legs, and cleaning a wound on her stomach. She lifts Clara's bed and gives her some liquid to drink. Clara looks around and realises she is in a different room. This one has a window. She can see the orange sky and dusty clouds.

"Where am I?" Her voice is a croak.

"In the clinic." The woman offers her more liquid.

"Now you are awake we can make you strong enough to leave."

"Leave?" Clara shakes her head. "I don't understand."

"You have been chosen. You will be living with an officer so once you are strong enough you will be dressed and taken to him."

"A child!" Clara tries to sit up, tugging at the straps. "A child? Was there a child, has it gone? Where is Elle?"

"I know no one called Elle." The woman pushes her back down. "As for the child. There will be no more children for you. Not in this life."

"Why? What have you done?" Clara can feel tears rising to her eyes.

"I have done nothing." The woman is leaving. "But you are one of them now. You've been prepared as they all are. The ability to have children has been removed. That is no longer a burden you have to concern yourself with."

As she leaves Clara feels a chill creep over her. She knows what has happened, and she also knows what her future will be when the officer tires of her. Her fate has been sealed.

Elle grows tired of watching the door for Clara's red head to appear. She withdraws into herself. Sitting silent for hours, feeling the growth of the child within her. When they are taken outside, she takes no interest; she stands in the corner of the yard against the solitary tree pushing its green leaves upwards, desperate to live and grow. She envies it. It is so determined to live. Unlike her. She has no real wish to live. Not to go back into the circle of horror that the breeding house represents.

Then one day it happens.

Something is moving; churning, turning inside her. She clutches her stomach and feels something push back. She stares at her own belly and sees it move. Inside the child is striving for life in the same way as the lonely tree. The maternal hormones that have neglected her thus far begin to flow and suddenly, from nowhere, the urge to protect, to nurture, to give life takes over her.

The nurses watch and smile to themselves. They see the change in her, a glow that comes to her pallid skin and the way in which she cradles herself and murmurs words of comfort to the child inside her. Good. This is good. The tall pale girl has a future here after all. The child will grow well, and, with luck, will be delivered safely and be strong.

CHAPTER 6

It has been two months since Clara nearly died in a pool of her own blood. Two months that she has lain in this white hospital room. The medics cannot understand why but she is still unable to walk without aid; she is thin and sad. Despite their best efforts they have been unable to take her to Aleric.

Footsteps sound in the hallway early one morning and the doctor looks over his shoulder. He knew this day would come.

"Well." Aleric stands in front of him, tall and broad. "Where is she?"

"Aleric, Sir." The doctor shakes his head. "Choose another. This one does not thrive. She cannot stand alone and gains no weight. There are many women, choose another."

Aleric looks into the room where Clara sleeps. Her red hair is tumbling over her pillow and her eyes are closed. Her skin is as pale as the sheets that cover her. The bones of her shoulders protrude. But even in this weak and debilitated state she stirs him and memories of her clinging to him run through his brain.

"Bring her to me." He commands. "Send a nurse with her if you must. Let us see if living in a decent space and good food will make a change."

"Very well." The doctor nodded. "If not?"

"You know the outcome." Aleric was already walking away.

The nurse in Clara's room overhears the conversation. She looks at her patient and feels a wave of pity. She hopes for her sake she can be strong; how sad would it be to pick such a flower when it is yet to bloom?

Aleric's rooms are outside the main government building; the large white palace flanked by four towers. Once it had been a place where kings and queens lived, now it housed the Great Council that ruled the army; the army that in turn ruled the land. His rooms are high up and overlook the city, the balcony has a fountain that plays a constant stream of water and there are a few green plants. The floors are white and clean and glass windows cover an entire wall filling the main room with light. He spends little time here. He will bathe and sleep here but eats with his men. That will have to change now. He will be expected to attend functions with the red-haired woman at his side. She will be dressed in the finest gowns, and he will make sure that he sources the most precious of gemstones for her. He feels a thrill of excitement.

Behind these doors where no one can see them they will live a different life. She will see him, all of him, and he will make her his own. To have whenever he desires. Reaching for a flask of amber liquid he pours himself a drink. She will be here soon. He must be ready.

The nurse brings Clara in a wheelchair. She is drowsy and not aware of her new surroundings. Aleric opens the door to the terrace and points.

"Put her out there in the air. Let her feel the sun on her skin. Then leave us."

The nurse frowns, she knows she should never question an order, but she is here to care for a patient.

"Sir."

She hesitates. "She still needs care."

"I know this." Aleric snaps. "Come back in one hour; you can tend to her then."

"Very well." The nurse leaves, with a lowered head.

Aleric turns to Clara who is staring with unseeing eyes at the city below her.

"Welcome." He lowers his voice. "I hope you remember me. This is your home now."

She nods and he sees a tear sliding a silver trail down her cheek.

"Why are you crying?" He shakes his head. "Look at what you have? This is all yours. You will have fine clothes, jewels, food."

"Freedom." Her voice is little more than a whisper. "I will not have my freedom."

Aleric studies her for a moment. He had expected her to be pleased, at the least, for her to turn to him with her green eyes and reach for him in gratitude. But she continues to stare and has yet to look in his direction.

"Look at me." He commands. "Look at me, woman, NOW!"

She turns her eyes on him; eyes void of life and interest.

"Yes?" She raises her chin.

"I have given you this." He waves his hand around him. "You should be pleased."

"You have also arranged my execution." Clara looks away again. "Why should I be pleased?"

"Very well." Aleric steps forward and pulls her face back to his. "If you persist in this behaviour that day will come sooner than you think."

"Good." For the first time a spark of life, a flicker of emotion in her eyes. "Better that than be your slave."

"I will leave you." Aleric pushes her away from him. "I will let you think on what you have said. When I return, I hope you will see that this is a good thing for you. It is an honour."

Clara hears him walk away and feels a sob tearing out of her body.

An honour.

An honour to be used at his bidding until she is no longer wanted and then to be slaughtered like an animal. If that is to be her end, then she will face it now and get it over with.

When the nurse returns Clara is asleep still sitting in the chair on the terrace. The nurse takes her inside and helps her into bed. She takes warm water and cleans her gently, and then encourages her to drink strong hot liquid to boost her strength.

"Please." She whispers. "Please fight. Don't give in and let them end you. You are young, you are beautiful, so many would love to have this. What is it, fulfilling the needs of a man when he feels the urge on him, when compared with this life that you can have. Remember the breeding houses. Remember the selections, the way you were treated. That is all over for you now. Please fight."

Clara opens her reddened eyes and looks at her. The nurse has a kind face and greying hair. Clara reaches up and touches her face and the woman catches her hand and squeezes it.

"Fight little one." She urges. "Eat, drink, be strong, live this life for all the poor souls out there who cannot ever live like this. The sick, the maimed, the ugly, the unwanted. When you rise every day think of them hiding in the hills or waiting for their time in the breeding house to end. Live for them."

Clara nods. Her mind wanders to the winters spent in the village, huddled together against the cold. She feels the smooth fresh sheets beneath her and remembers the worn blankets that used to serve as bedding. She thinks of Elle, for the first time in weeks and wonders where she is. The nurse is right, she cannot give up.

"My legs." She mumbles "I can't walk."

"You will." The Nurse looks over her shoulder, she cannot be heard. "The drug you took to end the pregnancy has made the lower half of your body weak. But it will return; you must keep trying to use them. Even when you are in bed, move your toes, your knees, to make them strong again."

"Thank you." Clara smiles.

"Be strong." The nurse lays a hand on her head. "Officer Aleric is a good man, not like the others. You will have a better life here. A life where you can help others."

As she walks away Clara's head races, full of thoughts. Help others? How? Could she provide a home for Elle? Could Elle come and be here with her? She has to learn, to watch, to listen, and find her way in this position she finds herself in. She hopes that the next time the Nurse comes they will be alone again, and she can ask questions of her. Somehow, she no longer feels completely alone.

Aleric returns when it is late. He has eaten with his men and shared ale with them. He is edgy and nervous; he is not used to sharing his rooms with another being. He is beginning to doubt his choice. When he walks into the room, he sees Clara in bed. But she is sitting up and looking out of the window at the darkening sky. A light flickers beside her and he can see a steaming mug of hot liquid in her hand.

"How do you feel?" His voice makes her jump.

"A little better." Her voice is hoarse.

"Good. Have you eaten?"

"No." Clara shakes her head. "The nurse brought me this to drink. It is enough."

"Good."

From here she cannot see the eyes behind the metal mask, but she knows that in the safety of his rooms he will reveal himself. She wants to see him, wants to see the man who she had clung to that day; the man she had wanted to return to her repeatedly. Before her own brother had rutted with her like a pig. But as she watches him Aleric hesitates. He is not ready to disclose himself yet. There is still some distance between them, something he cannot understand. Perhaps this was not the right choice to have made.

"Sleep well." He says and is gone.

For the next couple of days Aleric comes and speaks to her and then leaves. The days are long; she sits on the terrace and watches the city below her. In the evenings she looks up at the lights in the dark sky. The nurse brings her books, old books made of paper that have survived the war. She devours them hungrily as they provide her with an escape from her prison.

On the evening of the third day Aleric returns late in the evening. He finds her not in the bed but still on the terrace her head bent over a shabby old book. Beside her is a half-eaten piece of fruit and some bread.

"Good evening." He stands in the entrance to the terrace.

"Hello." Clara looks up at him. There is colour slowly returning to her cheeks. "Something happened today."

"Oh, yes? What was that."

"This." Slowly, with discomfort written all over her face Clara pulls herself awkwardly to her feet. Then she stands, unaided and with hands held in front of her, reaching for the table should she need it, and takes a few steps forward. As she reaches the table, she turns to him, and a half smile dances across her lips. Her face is lit with pleasure. He looks at her with her red hair swinging, the loose gown barely covering her pale breasts and feels his blood rushing. He walks forward and catches her arms, pulling her to him.

"Well done." She can hear the smile in his voice. "Can you walk to the bedroom?"

Clara hesitates. She is not ready for this; but

that, after all is why she is here.

"I don't think so." She murmurs. "Not yet."

"A shame." Aleric loosens her arms. "A pleasure we both could have enjoyed, I'm sure."

Clara narrows her eyes at him. Having his metal face that close to her makes her nervous; but from here she can see his eyes glinting. She reaches up and touches the cold hard metal.

"Who are you?" She whispers.

Aleric can smell the warmth of her skin, and the scent of her hair. Anger, frustration, and lust overcome him, and he sweeps her up into his arms and carries her into the bedroom. He throws her back on the bed and tugs at her gown; it lifts above her head to reveal her beautiful body, thinner than he remembers but no less tempting. Her eyes are scared but he can hear her breath quickening. He can see the pulse racing in her neck.

With swift fingers he removes his leather trousers, and he can feel her staring at his body. He bends over her and pulls her legs apart, diving swiftly into her. He lets out a groan as the sensation overcomes him. Slowly, slowly he starts to feel her move with him and then, there it is, the arms are reaching up for him, she is shuddering and gasping and clinging onto him. Through the metal of his mask, he sees her eyes are closed, head tilted back, then she looks at him as she feels him release. He stares back into her hazy eyes and sees her fingers touching the face of the mask.

Pulling backwards he kneels between her legs and reaches behind his head.

As Clara watches him remove the mask, she feels the cold grip of terror at her throat; the fear of the unknown takes over her. Then the metal mask falls away and she sees his face.

Aleric has golden hair, slicked back from his strong forehead and clear eyes that are somewhere between grey and pale blue. His cheekbones are high and proud above a strong jaw. There is stubble on his chin.

He is, after all, just a man. A beautiful, strong, living, breathing man.

Clara sits up and as her fingers trace the golden hair on his chest, shivers of ice run down his spine.

"I am Aleric." He catches her hand and in a gesture that completely throws her, lifts it to his lips.

"Clara. Or I was, once." She looks at the brand on her arm.

"Clara you will be again."

"What happens now?"

"What happens is while we are here, I have no need of this." He casts the mask onto the floor. "We will eat together, talk together, and share a bed. In all ways. When I need to attend some celebrations, you will accompany me. In some cases, I will wear that, in some I will not. Sometimes you need to be veiled. For your own safety."

"And when you are not here?"

"Do as you will." Aleric shrugs. "But you can never leave alone. You must always be accompanied and wear a veil."

"I can go outside?"

"Yes. Within the confines of the city. But only that. The brand will make sure you don't leave."

"The brand? How?"

"Inside the brand there is a chip. If you try to leave you will be ended; instantly."

Slowly Clara regains her strength.

Aleric provides her, as she had imagined, with clothes and jewels. She bathes every day in deep scented baths ready for his return. They never talk about what he does when he is gone, only about their life together, such as it is. Every night Aleric takes her, but it is no chore to her now. She finds it as satisfying as he and together they discover each other's bodies in ways that only serve to increase the pleasure.

When they sleep Aleric lies close, an arm over her body and she learns to curl into him, her head resting on his muscular chest. One day she wakes and finds him looking at her and as she smiles, he bends his head and kisses her on the lips. This has never happened before; she hesitates then returns the kiss, her body arching with longing.

A selection in a breeding house is starting

to flower into something more; something unbeknown to either of them. Something called love.

CHAPTER 7

The pains start in the middle of the night, accompanied by a sudden soaking of all her undergarments. In the dark recesses of the room Elle shouts for help. One of the women comes to her aid.

"It's okay." She pats Elle's hand, her own belly bulging with her late term pregnancy. "Your baby is on the way. Nothing to be afraid of."

But Elle is afraid; the pains wracking her body are unexpected, she cannot sit up, or stand and wants to scream and groan.

She has seen too many women taken away who never come back.

She is afraid of the birth.

She is afraid of the death that may follow.

She is afraid.

The medics arrive shortly after and take Elle to a long room filled with beds; on each is a woman birthing a child. Some are screaming and gasping for air, some are silent and staring into space, others lie in blood-stained sheets and have bidden the world goodbye. There is no help here; The strong survive, the weak die. Nothing to ease the pain or make the birthing easier. The medics attend purely to ensure the safe delivery of the child; the mother has fulfilled her purpose. There are other women laden with milk who will take their place and use the baby to replace their own lost infant.

They lay Elle on a bed and place wires on her stomach and her arms. They attach a drip to her vein to speed up the birthing and set up machines beside her. Then with just one nurse to watch over her and many others they leave.

The pains increase once the fluid enters her body; they become stronger and more frequent until she is soaked with sweat and screaming, straining desperately to move position and find relief.

"Push" The nurse tells her." Don't fight it just push."

But Elle is exhausted. A red film crosses her eyes, and she begins to drift into unconsciousness. The nurse rouses her, shaking her vigorously.

"Stay awake." She whispers. "Stay awake and push, or they will cut you."

Her eyes dart to the end of the room where the medics are approaching a woman with a trolley. A scream of pain unlike anything Elle has ever heard fills the room.

"You see." The nurse strokes her head. "They will cut you, stay awake and keep pushing."

Through her blurred eyes Elle can see a pool of blood on the floor and a child in a nurse's arms; the mother lies still underneath a scarlet sheet. She grips the side of the bed with her hands and pulls herself up, bending forward she grits her teeth and pushes.

"That's it." The nurse encourages her. "Keep going."

The red haze is coming back; and as she pushes Elle feels a spasm run through her body and she collapses back on the sheets shuddering. Then she feels a pulling sensation between her legs; something is being dragged out of her. The pains dull and begin to fade, and she feels a weight laying on her sweat soaked stomach. Opening her eyes, fighting the nausea that overwhelms her she looks down and sees a tiny figure topped with a crown of dark hair; and two dark eyes.

"A boy." The nurse is relieved. "Well done."

She bends low to Elle and whispers in her ear.

"You had a fit. You must lie very still until the medics check you; I pulled the child from you; it was the only way to help."

Elle nods and looks at her.

"Thank you." She whispers. It is over. The child is here; the fear is leaving her. She feels weak and ill but for now she can lie here, and rest wrapped in the comforting red haze that surrounds her.

Elle lies there for a few more days until she is strong enough to move. The nurses tend to her baby. They turn her to her side to feed him and gradually she grows accustomed to the feeling of him suckling. It is only her plentiful milk and her ability to feed the child herself that keeps her alive. Her strength returns and one day they sit her upright. Her head spins and she feels wave after wave of giddiness, but she grits her teeth and forces herself through the fog that envelops her. In a few hours she is on her feet and soon she is taken to a room where she will live with other nursing mothers. This room is light and has air flowing through it. There are cribs for the babies and the mothers have access to showers and bathing units for the babies. The food is good here; there is fruit, vegetables, and meat. There is a small courtyard where the women stand barefoot, babes on their hips, looking out through the railings at the metal-faced men going about their day. They all wonder which is the man that fathered the child in their arms. Do they care? Do they ever look at the women and wonder which of the bundles of rags is their child?

From their viewpoint on the edge of squalor they see the great houses of the city, the Grand Palace of the Government, and every day they see trucks bringing more women to the breeding houses.

Elle calls her baby Baelar. It was her father's name. She knows that they may choose another name for him but to her he is Baelar. She sings to him. Her voice is soft and soothing, and the other mothers sit close listening, their own children calmed by Elle's gentle voice. She sings songs that she remembers from her childhood; songs her mother sang. The words bring tears to the eyes of the women; and to those of the nurses that watch over them as they remember their own childhood. A time before their lives were dominated by the men in metal masks who want to rule and control the planet.

Baelar grows stronger every day; he is always hungry and as he grows fatter Elle grows thinner. She takes to sitting close to the gates and watching the world outside. One day she sees flags flying and banners lining the front of the Palace building.

"What's going on?" She asks the nurse who is checking Baelar over.

"A presentation." The nurse shrugs. "Some man is being made a general. You will see them soon. All clad in their finery while we sit here in the dust like animals."

The tone in her voice makes Elle look up. There is bitterness spread across her face. She smiles at Elle and places a hand on her head.

"Don't ever think you are alone. We may do their work, but it is not the work that we would choose to do. Sometimes, to stay alive, we all have to do things we don't want to."

"I know." Elle reaches up and takes her hand. "We are all prisoners here."

"Even him." The nurse looks down at Baelar. "He is free now, but the day will come when all he will see is life from inside a metal mask. He will forget everything but the orders he has to carry out."

Elle hugs Baelar tightly. The thought of him leaving her brings tears to her eyes. In the dirt, in the misery, in the dreary bleakness of her existence, he is all she draws breath for.

The vehicles bringing the guests start arriving at what would be noon if the sky was clear. They reflect the weak grains of light that fall on them and from them emerge the officers and their women. The women are healthy and well dressed; they cling to the leather arms of their men. The other women in the dust filled yard huddle at the gates; wretches in ragged garments cradling the next generation of the army in their arms. Sometimes the women in fine clothes look at them in shock as if the sight reminds them of what really causes the wheels of this army's machinery to turn. They all turn away quickly, some in disgust, some in pity; all in fear.

A vehicle pulls up in front of the gates and a tall man with a metal mask that glints like gold gets out of it. His shoulders are broad, and he holds out his hand to help his woman from the vehicle. She wears an emerald green dress with a gold veil to compliment the shimmering gleam of his metal face. Despite her veil her eyes are visible, as is her hair.

Long, lustrous curls of deep red hair.

"Clara!" Elle leaps to her feet and shakes the railings. "Clara! Clara it's me!"

But the woman is walking away, her arm through that of the officer beside her. Only as she reaches the steps to the Palace does she hesitate. Her head turns slightly as she looks about her; before she walks on and through the doors.

Clara sits through the ceremony with her stomach churning. Aleric is to be made a general. It is the first time she has accompanied him to an occasion such as this and she feels awkward. The gown he has brought her is beautiful and the silk caresses her skin as she walks. They sit side by side and watch the speeches and the demonstrations of how powerful the army is. She looks at him and can just see through the gleam of his new golden metal face the outline of his cheekbones. A tingle runs through her. The awkwardness disappears and a warm glow heats her skin. This is her man. He chose her. Their life together is comfortable; they talk, he holds her in his arms and strokes her hair. This man who is about to be honoured chose her as his companion. She turns her eyes back to the platform and as she does, so she feels Aleric's hand brushing against hers. A half smile dances over her veiled lips. She cannot wait for this to be over; for the food and drink that follows to be done so that they can go home. The thought makes her catch her breath.

Home. For that is what it has become.

As the speeches drag on something begins to niggle at Clara's brain. As she had been getting out of the car, she had seen the women in worn stained clothes behind the gates, each one cradling a child in their arms. She had heard her name. More than once. As she sits and thinks backwards the realisation hits her and she gasps.

Aleric looks at her as others turn in their direction. She lowers her head quickly and murmurs an apology.

It was Elle who had called her name. Elle had been one of the ragged women; her child would have been born by now. Elle who she had promised to always stay with. Elle, who had given birth and was nursing a child while she, Clara, spent her days reclining on a chair reading or being massaged and pampered. What was she becoming? Elle was her friend; they had been through the days of the war together and she had forgotten her. Unbiddcn a tear slides down her cheek and a leather clad hand reaches out to wipe it away. Clara stares ahead, forcing herself to watch what is going on and to play her part. She cannot let Aleric down. Without him she has nothing. There is no breeding house for her now. This is all she will ever have.

Aleric receives his presentation and listens to the applause that echoes through the hall. He is proud of what he has achieved. He can move himself and Clara into one of the houses at the outskirts of the city where there is a garden, and she can walk with her maids and not be confined to the rooms they currently share. But there is something that worries him; something he will need to talk to her about and soon. It has already been mentioned that he has not been seen in the breeding houses since he took Clara as his companion. As a general he will be even more expected to sire the soldiers of the future. The thought of being with a woman other than Clara fills him with no pleasure; but it is a duty he must fulfil. How Clara will take the knowledge that he must give himself to others he is not sure. Theirs is a passion unlike anything he has known. This beautiful red headed woman is changing his life.

Clara waits at Aleric's side while he greets the Council and receives their praise. There will be a feast at the governor's house after the reception. There she can remove her veil and enjoy the food and drink on offer. The veil irritates her. But before that she must somehow see into the courtyard of dirt and find Elle. Her mind is working fast; Aleric is talking of a house they will move to, with a garden; surely Elle could come and live there with them? Someone to help fill the lonely hours when Aleric is gone. She looks at the tall man beside her. He is kind, he will understand that she cannot leave her friend in that dire place. Somehow when they leave, she must indicate to Elle that she has heard her.

But when they leave the courtyard is empty. Only dust fills the footprints that are left behind.

Germin stands at the back of the crowded auditorium and watches the presentation. He watches Aleric receive his generals' stripes and sees him return to his seat. As he sits, he reaches out to the woman beside him and lays his hand on her shoulder. Germin knows who sits behind the veil. He has seen the red hair partially hidden by the gold lace. The woman he now knew to be his sister. The familiar knot of nerves rolls in his stomach.

Ever since that night it has haunted him. If it comes into his head, he feels sickness in his stomach and a cold sensation on his skin. The memory cannot, however hard he tries, be erased. He has been to the breeding houses many times since and has sired children, he knows that. But he had never known what had become of his sister and if there had been a child.

Now he knew. Aleric had claimed her for himself.

Germin understood what they did to the women who were companions. There would be no childbearing for her. He also knew what happened to the women at the end of their time. When that time came, he would be there. It would have to be he, Germin, who would save her. It was the only way to cleanse himself of this guilt.

CHAPTER 8

The room is dark, only the lights from the city outside give her eyes a path to the window.

"You what?" Clara is still. Her back, he can see, is rigid and tense.

"I am going to the breeding houses. It is expected of me." Aleric's voice is sharper than he intends.

"Why?" Clara speaks through gritted teeth. "Am I not enough for you?"

"Clara!" Aleric lays a hand on her shoulder, and she snatches it away. "You know that is not the case. It is required of me, particularly now."

She turns to look at him. She has twisted her hair into a knot at the back of her head, a few strands fall around her slender neck. The black silk underwear shows off the pale gold of her skin. Her eyes glitter pale and fierce in her proud face.

"So, what do I do while you are away for, how long? Four nights? Five? Sit home and wait for you to return then welcome you back into my bed with open arms and legs?"

"Enough!" Aleric grabs her arms and shakes her. "Enough of this. You know the law, the way it is. This is what I am, what we are. You are here only because I want you to be, remember that."

"Cast me out then!" She tugs herself free of him. "End it. Go on! The proud general will have a selection of women wanting to share their days with him."

Aleric stares at her, her trembling lips, her heaving chest and takes a deep breath. She stares back at his golden hair, his broad shoulders, and his proud, strong face. Before she can open her mouth to speak, he has swept her up in his arms and is carrying her to the bedroom.

"I will show you." He speaks softly in her ear. "I will show you what those women you speak of would all love to have."

Throwing her roughly on the bed he kneels over her for a second before his hands roughly part her legs.

"Go on." She taunts him. "Show me what the mighty general can do."

As Aleric plunges hard inside her she throws her head back and groans. Harder and harder he punishes her with his body, one hand clutching at her hair, another holding one leg high above his shoulder until she is gasping for breath.

"Aleric!" She whimpers. "Please."

"Please what?" He pauses and feels her writhing

beneath him.

She is watching him with wide eyes.

"You are hurting me."

"Am I?" Another thrust, another tug at her tangled hair.

"Yes."

"If this is how you want to be treated, this is how you will be treated." His lips are close to her ear.

She turns her head and for a second feels him brush them on her cheek.

"Listen to me," he whispers. "I do not want to do what I have to do; but it's what I am. This is different. This has…"

"Has what?"

"Meaning."

His head falls onto her shoulder and when he speaks his voice is muffled.

"I should not say this to you Clara, this is not what it should be, but you mean something to me. I will not cast you out. I want you to be here, to be at my side; but I have to do what is expected of me or we will both suffer for it."

Clara closes her eyes and slowly wraps the one raised leg around his back pulling him down tightly to her.

"Promise me," she whispers as they begin to move together. "Never look another woman in the eye when you do this. Only me."

"Only you."

Clara sits at the edge of the bed and watches Aleric. He is half asleep, one strong arm laying across his stomach.

"There is one thing." She hesitates, unsure of his reaction should she proceed.

"What." Aleric doesn't open his eyes.

"There was a girl, a friend, she was brought here with me. She was with child. When we went to the presentation, I thought I heard her call my name. She was there, with all the other women with children. Can you find her for me?"

"What?" Aleric sits up and rubs his hair. "Clara, that is almost impossible, you know that. Why do you want me to do this? If I were to find her, what would you want me to do?"

"Bring her to me. In our new home. She can be a maid, safe, away from the men. Aleric you are different, you don't know what they do."

"You ask too much. It is beyond my power Clara."

"No. You as an officer had me sterilised so that you could bring me here. You are a general now. This is a small thing, a maid for your house. Surely you can do that."

"It's impossible. Women only leave the breeding house when they can no longer breed."

"Or they take the eye of an officer." Clara's snort

of disgust is loud. "Maybe General Aleric can say he wants two women."

"Two." Aleric laughs suddenly. "By whatever gods there are Clara you are enough woman for any man. I will ask some questions. When I can. That is all I can say."

Clara lays back on the pillows and a half smile plays across her lips. It is a start. Turning onto her side she lays her head on Aleric's chest. She can smell the warmth of his skin. Closing her eyes, she tries to forget what the future will be for them. She has to think only of this, now. This moment and nothing more. Not breeding houses, or the other women inside them, or the day when the man beside her will turn his eyes onto another.

CHAPTER 9

Elle stands in the corner of the courtyard and looks out onto the street. Baelar is mewling quietly at her breast. She stares at the grand white building in front of her and remembers the crowd that had gathered a few days previously. She has learned that the man Clara had been with, the man with the golden face, had been made a general. So that's where Clara had ended up. Away from here and the grim cries of babies and the smell of soiled nappies. She was one of the chosen ones, women who had fine clothes and scent. Did she enjoy it, Elle wondered, having to accommodate the man every night or whenever his attention turned to her. She had walked into the building with her arm through his and something about the closeness between them made Elle think that perhaps she did. Tears moisten her eyelashes. How their lives have changed in eleven short months. She looks at Baelar, a down of hair on his head, his eyes closed peacefully. He is a handsome child and Elle wonders, not for the first time, what the man who had made him looked like. She knows her time with him is short; that as soon as he can eat food other than her milk, he will be taken away from her. Then she will go back to the breeding house and begin the cycle again. The tears fall. Her body is still recovering from the birthing; the red haze returns occasionally and makes her weak. She does not know if her body will take the ordeal again.

"Elle." One of the nurses is behind her. "What is wrong?"

"It will be time soon. They will take him away."

"Yes, but he will be well cared for, and you know he will have a good life."

"But not a life with me."

"No. Not with you."

"The man who was made general. The woman with him was my friend. Before we were brought here, we grew up together."

The nurse sighs. She has seen this before.

"She looked happy. Who is he?"

"That is General Aleric. He is one of the better ones, so I am told. He has never claimed a woman for a companion before this."

"So," Elle sniffs back the tears. "He must like my friend a lot."

"Perhaps. Perhaps it is something he has had to do. But it won't stop him from visiting the breeding houses; it is even more important now that he sires children."

"That won't be nice." Elle looks at her. "How will

she feel about that I wonder."

"She will accept it." The nurse lays her hand on her shoulder. "They all do."

"Why couldn't it have been me." Elle's face draws with anguish. "No more breeding houses. No more birthing."

"Don't be too jealous. "The nurse pats her gently. "When her time with him is over, so will be her life. She will know too much. They never leave once they enter that world."

"What do you mean?"

"She will die." The nurse nods grimly. "That way all the secrets she hears are protected. No, my child, this way you have a chance, a chance to live many years; your friend does not. Her days have been numbered."

Elle stares at her as she walks away; sickness rising in her throat. This cannot be happening. Does Clara know? Somehow, they have to find each other and be together again before it is too late.

Aleric stands at the doorway of the breeding house and hesitates. He has no desire to do this. He has left Clara tearful in their bed. But it is his duty. He will do no more than he must. His time here will be swift, and he will leave as soon as it is done. He does not even care which woman he has; he has no desire to choose. As he walks into the gloomy corridor, he hears the cries of babies in the distance. What had Clara told him? That her friend was here somewhere. Maybe finding her would ease the guilt he felt at that moment. They would move soon to the house he had chosen; he would not be able to spend as much time with Clara then so a maid, a female companion would be useful. He would ask questions, find out when the child would be weaned and hopefully bring the woman to Clara.

The door opens. They are bringing out the women for selection. He casts his eyes over them; sorry wretches scrubbed clean for his pleasure. There is a young girl with dark hair; she looks barely old enough to be here and another who must surely be close to ending her time in the houses. He raises his hand and points at a woman with pale gold hair similar to his own. She was pleasant enough to encourage him to perform the act. He watches her as she is pushed ahead of him and takes a deep breath. He would make this as swift as possible.

Clara stands on the balcony and looks down on the vehicles moving along the road. She knows where he is. He would normally be here by now ready to dine.

"Your dinner Madam." The maid comes in carrying a covered plate.

"Put it there." Clara nods at the table. "I have no appetite."

She watches the maid as she is about to go and

then calls after her.

"Wait. Have you eaten?"

"No Madam."

"Don't call me that. My name is Clara, come we will eat this together."

"What? I can't. What would happen to me if anyone knew?"

"Who will know?" Clara is at the table. "I will say nothing, and the general will not be home early tonight."

The maid glances at the steaming plate of food and her mouth begins to water. She looks at Clara and hesitates.

"Please." Clara takes a seat. "You will be helping me, and I should imagine that it has been a long time since you ate a meal like this."

"In truth," the girl blushes, "I have never had a meal like this."

They eat together and Clara finds the girl starts to relax and they talk. The girl was brought into the city with her mother; the mother, she believes, was sent to the breeding houses, she was sent to a building where the clothes of the soldiers were cleaned. She was moved to the rooms of the officers as a maid when she was eighteen. The doctors had carried out tests on her and stated that she would never be fit to have children.

"I was pleased." The girl reaches for more bread. "But scared, as I didn't know what would happen to me. Then they said they needed new maids in the quarters of the officers, so they sent me here. I hope I can stay here. I have food and a clean place to sleep. No man will ever come near me as I have no use."

"What of your mother?" Clara is drinking too much wine and can feel her head starting to spin.

"I don't know." The girl shook her head. "I think she must be dead by now."

"I'm sorry." Clara reaches out and takes her hand. "One day, I hope, things will change, and we will all see our families again."

The girl looks over her shoulder her face tense with nerves.

"There's no one there." Clara smiles reassuringly. "But now, maybe you should go before you are missed. Come tomorrow. If I am alone again, we can talk some more."

It is hours later that Clara hears the door open and the booted feet of Aleric come into the room. She is lying on a chair in the darkness; an empty flagon of wine beside her. She hears Aleric undressing and then the sound of water running as he cleans himself.

"Well." Her voice is bitter. "What was she like?"

Aleric takes a deep breath before he answers.

"She was acceptable. Quiet, submissive."

"Did you enjoy her?"

"I wasn't there to enjoy myself. I was there to

complete a job which I did."

Clara has got to her feet and is standing behind him. He smells the wine on her breath.

"It is late." He tells her. "I must sleep."

"Yes." She staggers slightly. "You need more energy for tomorrow."

"Clara." Aleric stands before her, naked, and she averts her eyes; the knowledge of someone else sharing his body cuts at her like a knife. "This cannot happen every time. This does not affect us."

"Oh, but it does." Clara walks past him into the bedroom. "It affects us in every way."

"No, it doesn't." Aleric stands over her. "Not unless you let it."

She is sliding into the sheets, and he sits beside her. The sight of the sheet draping over her curving hips makes heat rush through his body.

"You see." He lifts the sheet and slips in beside her. "It does not affect us at all. I will always come back to you."

Clara looks up at him, he can see defiance in her eyes.

"Until the next woman takes your eye."

"Is that what you are afraid of, being replaced?"

"No!" Clara sits abruptly upright. "I hate the fact that tonight you have been with someone else. They have felt you, and right now this very minute they could be with child. *Your* child: the child I can never have."

Aleric lays back and stares at the ceiling.

"What would you prefer? To be here with me every day or to have a child that would be taken away from you that you would never see again? This will last; far longer than a few brief months with a child."

He raises his hand and strokes her tumbling mane of hair.

"Lie by me." He commands. Clara lies down slowly, her body still rigid with resistance.

"The woman with the child."

"Elle." Clara hisses. "Her name is Elle."

"I will ask some questions. I will try and ensure she comes to the house with us; but it has to be after the child is weaned and not before."

Clara imagines a child, a child she could hold and sing to, a child to walk with in the gardens. The image overwhelms her and when she turns to him he sees that her eyes are full of tears.

"Why? Why not before?"

"His future is planned, and she has no part in it. Nor do we."

CHAPTER 10

The day that they take Baelar from her Elle screams and throws herself at the soldiers.

"Bastards!" She cries. "You soulless pitiful bastards! Bring him back to me!"

But they push her aside and take the wailing baby, giving him to the waiting nurse. One of the soldiers, narrower in the hips, less burly, hangs back.

"He will be fine." He murmurs, low enough that only she can hear. "I will watch out for him."

"Why?" Elle is gasping for breath; she feels an iron hand clutching at her throat, the panic threatening to overwhelm her. "Why would you do that?"

A thought breaks into her muddled brain, and she looks at him, watching the faint movement of eyes behind the metal mask.

"Are you, his father?"

"No." There is laughter in his voice. "I am not."

"Then who are you? Why would you care what happens to him?"

His voice is so low she can barely hear him despite being so close.

"I am Germin." He whispers. "And I have many wrongs to put right in this life."

As he walks away Elle feels a wave of weakness wash over her. Germin? Could it be? She remembers Clara, rocking and sobbing, distraught with grief. The same Germin who had unwittingly chosen his own sister at the breeding houses was going to watch over her child? Her mind chases split second thoughts around in circles. Is this good? Does she trust him to watch over her precious boy? But then, what else can she do, who else does she know that could make sure Baelar grows and is well? He is at the door and as he goes to leave, he looks back at her, there is an almost imperceptible nod, and then he is gone.

The walk back to the breeding houses is long and miserable. All around her women are weeping for lost children; all are realising that they must start the torrid process again. They will be scrubbed clean and placed on parade. The children had given them not only comfort but safety. Safety from the breeding houses and all that followed. As they enter the first building one of the soldiers at the gate steps forward and clutches Elle's arm.

"Not you." He commands. "You are to come with me."

"What? Why?" Elle tugs back at him, fear making her bold enough to dispute his authority.

"Just come." He pushes her roughly ahead of him.

This corridor is not one she has walked before; it leads away from the breeding houses towards the official buildings. Then suddenly they are outside. There is a breeze that touches her skin and makes her shiver. There is a vehicle ahead of them. A stab of terror hits Elle in the gut. Where were they taking her? Was this it? Was this the end of it all?

The door of the vehicle opens and a tall, broad man in a gold mask steps out. He steps back and points inside. Elle stares at him as she passes. This is the general who had been with Clara. What did he want with her?

Then as she steps up into the vehicle, she sees a veiled face, with clear green eyes staring at her. Eyes wet with tears. From behind the veil tumbles a lock of red hair; hair she would recognise anywhere. She sits and stares, staring, unbelieving, wanting to speak, to cry, to shout, but the general is back in the vehicle and has taken the other seat opposite her. As she watches she sees him look at Clara. She can see the glint of his eyes behind his mask and could swear that he smiles as he lays his hand on Clara's leg.

The journey is short and takes them to a building surrounded by a high wall and metal gates. There is a garden, where the green of plants and the colours of flowers are starting to reclaim the earth. There is a courtyard with a fountain and the house has windows that look out onto it. The general gets out first and Elle watches in amazement as he lifts his hand to help Clara down. She steps down herself; and walks behind them, he is leading her friend back into the house, her arm is linked through his. Once inside he nods his head to Clara, a gesture that is almost a bow, and then is gone. Once the door has closed Clara removes her veil and stares at her friend.

"Elle." She begins to sob.

Elle stares at her, at the lavish house, the satin gown, the jewels and does not see the girl that she had loved. She sees a beautiful woman, a stranger, but a stranger who is holding out her arms to her. She shakes her head, not wanting to admit the changes that have taken place. She is ragged and dirty, her body aching for the baby that until that morning she had been feeding. Clara has grown into a great beauty, elegant, groomed, refined. They are worlds apart now, then she remembers the words of the Nurse at the birthing house. Clara may have beauty and finery, but she has a death sentence hanging over her; she is waiting for the day that the man in the gold mask tires of her. She takes a hesitant step forward and finds herself wrapped in the arms of the one true friend she has known.

Many hours later they are still sitting in the courtyard sharing their stories. Clara feels Elle's pain at losing her child, while Elle understands

Clara's pain at knowing she will never experience the warmth of a child in her arms. Each has their own struggle to carry through life and neither knows how long that life will last. When Elle reveals that Germin has promised to watch over Baelar she waits and wonders what Clara's reaction will be. Clara stares into space and takes a deep breath before speaking.

"I am glad. Baelar will have someone who knows his blood to watch over him. What happened between Germin and I, well, I will never forget it, but I know that he had no idea what he was doing. Perhaps this is his way of making amends."

"I think so." Elle reached out and laid a hand on her arm.

Clara looked down and saw how worn and grained with dirt Elle's hands were; nails broken; skin chapped.

"A bath." She gets to her feet. "We must get you a bath and I will find you some clothes."

When Aleric comes home later that evening, he finds the two of them dining at the table accompanied by the maid. They are all laughing. The woman, Elle, is wearing one of Clara's day gowns and her hair is now pale gold having been washed. Her skin is pale, and she is thin, but she already bears the glow of one who is warm and comfortable. He hesitates in the doorway. There is a part of him that doesn't want to disturb them; but the part of him that is a trained soldier remembers his position and what is expected of him.

He coughs.

The maid leaps to her feet and scurries to the kitchen to fetch his food. Elle rises, uncertain and bows her head.

"Aleric." Clara walks to him. "How lovely does Elle look now?"

Aleric stares at her through his gold mask. Normally he would pull this cage off himself and swoop her up in his arms but this stranger in his home made him hesitate.

"Are you not going to remove your mask?" Clara whispers.

"No. I am going to eat in our room, then bathe."

Clara frowns as he walks away.

"I am sorry." Elle mumbles. "I have upset him."

"No." Clara takes her arm. "He will be fine; he is used to having me to himself that is all."

"Well for now he shall." Elle places a kiss on her cheek. "I am here to work and work I will. You go to him, and I will go and help clear the dinner things in the kitchen. Sweet dreams Clara."

Aleric is standing looking out of the window.

He is naked apart from a white towel that clings to his hips. She slides up behind him and wraps her arms around his body, pressing herself into his back.

"Thank you." Her mouth covers his back in kisses.

"Just remember." He turns to face her. "She is here as a maid and a companion for the days; when I come home, I do not expect to find her and all the staff sitting to dinner with you."

"Well." Clara steps back, affronted. "If I knew when you would be home, I could make sure it didn't happen but as I never know, what am I to do, sit in silence?"

Aleric takes her face in his hands and forces her to look at him.

"Listen to me. In this house I am myself, but I am still a general, things still have to be obeyed. Things that you learn from me can never be shared. So, when I am here it is just you and I."

"But you can remove your mask in front of her? You do so in front of our maid."

"Our maid never leaves this house, and never will. This woman you want as a companion will walk out with you, and you are close, that I can see. She can never see me. It is not done."

"Why?"

"Those are the laws." Aleric shrugs. "My face is for you and for those close to me in my role as general. To see me unmasked will mean a certain death for her should anything happen to me; or you."

"You mean when I die, she will too?" Clara spits

out the words, unable to keep the venom from her voice. "In that case keep your face hidden General Aleric, the death of one woman on your hands is enough."

CHAPTER 11

The tension between them lasts for days. Clara spends her days with Elle, walking the streets and looking at the other houses, the gardens, the women who walk from them and the maids who accompany them. No children, anywhere, these women were all like her, doomed to death when the men who had claimed them grew tired of their charms. The more she thought about it the angrier she became; what right had Aleric to do this to her? He could have left her in the breeding houses with the other women, to become old and haggard and wipe the floors of the urinals at the end of her days. Instead, she was a prize, a trophy, which would tarnish and rust and be cast aside. Now she has condemned Elle to be tied to her fate. Elle watches her friend, unaware, and tries to cheer her but knows it is a battle that she is losing.

Aleric stays away from the house as much as possible; by day he works training the soldiers, by night he attends the breeding houses, he finds his anger at Clara manifesting itself in violence towards the women he chooses. He is rough with them, never cruel but harsh and knows that he hurts them as he breeds with them. He cares not, his only care is for the woman at home with whom he has not shared a bed for over a week. If she does not satisfy him there then what good is she to him? Maybe the time to choose a successor is coming closer; and far sooner than he ever thought possible.

On the evening of the fifth night Aleric comes home and finds Elle alone in the garden.

"Where is your mistress?" he asks abruptly.

"She has taken to her bed." The girl is softly spoken and sweet faced. "She feels unwell."

"Does she." Aleric sits on the chair and spreads his legs in front of him. "I return and she is not here to greet me. So why do I come? Why is she here?"

"Because you wanted her to be." Elle shakes her head at him. "She is your choice after all."

"For now." Aleric is desperate to remove his mask. "But choices can change."

"Please don't do that." Elle falls to her knees before him. "She is all the family I have. And I hers apart from..."

"Apart from what?" Aleric leans forward and she can see the pale glint of his eyes through the mask.

"Her brother." Elle pauses, unsure of what he knows.

"Brother?" Aleric rubs his hand over the metal that covers his face as if it can ease the ache within it.

"Where is he, this brother?"

"Here. He is a soldier."

"Is he now? And how do you know this?"

Elle lowers her head; she has already said too much.

"He was taken when he was a boy. So, he must be here."

"If he survived. What is his name?"

Elle hesitates.

"I am sorry sir; it was many years ago now I can't remember."

Aleric looks at her and knows that there is something she is not telling him.

"You are wrong." He gets to his feet. "She has no need of family. She has me. I am all she should need."

Elle watches him walk away and feels her heart pounding; she must learn to be more careful, what would the outcome be if he discovered what had happened with Germin and Clara; what would become of Baelar if Germin was not there to watch over him? She must learn to watch and listen and never speak, that way they could all stay safe.

Aleric stands in the doorway and watches Clara

sleeping. One strap of her silken nightshift has fallen off her shoulder. He feels something inside him twist and realises it is sorrow. This is what matters, this woman lying in the bed. His woman. All he wants is her, above everything else. Slowly he peels off his clothes and slips into the sheets beside her. Sliding his hand over her waist he lays his cheek on her silken back and falls asleep.

In the days that follow Aleric is away from the house for many hours allowing the women to share memories and daydream about how their lives may have been if the war had never happened.

"We would have been happy," Elle says one day as she kneads bread in the kitchen. "Happy and free."

Clara looks down at her hands, smooth and silken, her nails long and elegant. It's been a long time since her nails had been bitten with worry and filled with grime. She looks in the mirror hanging on the wall beside her and frowns. There is a hint of a wrinkle about her eyes. She must go to the beauty houses and have her face tended to. No one, apart from Aleric, Elle, and a few of the higher-ranking officers and their women know what she looks like beneath her veil, but she worries when signs of age start to appear. She knows full well her days with Aleric are not guaranteed to last forever.

"I said." Elle interrupts her thoughts. "Do you think we will ever be happy?"

"I am happy." Clara gives a soft smile. "At least happy enough and so should you be."

Elle stares at her.

"You are happy? Here? Living like this?"

"I am," Clara nods." Why should I not be? I have a warm house, food, fine clothes, and a man who cares for me."

"Clara!" Elle is aghast. "You are a trophy! Nothing more. Remember the chip in your brand? You are not free; you are a slave. We are both slaves. Slaves to the men who hide their faces in metal masks!"

"It is more than that." Clara shakes her head. "We have freedom here, Aleric is not like the other men, he lets you and I live as equals. We walk the streets, and we have freedom; we eat together and sit in the light and read together."

"When he isn't here." Elle snorts. "When he is here your wonderful Aleric makes sure I know my place."

"He has to." Clara shrugs. "It is just the way it is; even if he does not want to, he has to be seen to behave in the way expected of him."

"Even by siring children?"

There is silence.

"Yes."

Elle stares at her friend and shakes her head.

"What have you become Clara?"

"A woman who knows when she has the best life she can have." Clara gets to her feet. "In the world that we live in."

"And don't you want to change that world anymore?"

Clara stares out of the window and sees Aleric's vehicle approaching. The girl who would have fought to change everything is buried somewhere deep inside her. She is still there, lying dormant in her mind, but she no longer fights to get out.

"Sometimes." Clara looks back at Elle over her shoulder. "Then I wake and realise I have been dreaming."

Elle watches as she goes to meet Aleric. Sees the way that she reaches up to him and he lowers his head towards her. He will not remove his mask while she, Elle, is present but she has seen him once, when he was unaware of her presence, and she has seen the golden hair and strong jaw. She has seen all the reasons why her friend would want to stay here and live this fantasy, why she walks with her arm through his back into the house.

But she, Elle, still dreams of the village and the mountains and a life free of men. She will not stop wanting to change the world. Or the future that she knows awaits herself, her friend, and the child she can no longer see.

CHAPTER 12

Baelar sits and stares at the clothes in front of him.

He knew this day would come but he still is not prepared for it.

The day he would stop being a boy in a boy's uniform and start wearing the clothes that would bring the first transition into being a man and then onwards to becoming a soldier.

The clothes look hard and uncomfortable, dark leather and tall boots. Instead of the full metal mask that the men wear he will wear a hood and a mask over his nose and mouth. No need to cover his face entirely, just enough so that he is hidden from those around him. In the corner the soldier who is always there stands and watches. Every day since the one in which he had spoken his first words Baelar had known he was there. Watching, silent, always in the shadows, until the day that the lessons first began and then he would walk at Baelar's side and give him help, guidance, tips on how to defeat his opponents. Baelar wonders if the man is his father. He must have a father; all the young men here do, but none knew which of the soldiers had sired them. What other reason could there be for this man to always be present?

All Baelar knows is that his name is Germin.

Baelar stands, growing tall now after twelve years in this place. and begins to don the uniform in front of him.

Germin watches him and feels a glow of pride. The boy will do well. He will join the ranks of the academy and cover himself with glory. He is strong and determined; and on his walks Germin will get word to Elle through the ladies that grace the parks that her child flourishes and is becoming a handsome man. Germin has not seen Clara for many years. He knows that General Aleric still keeps her at his house and that Elle is still her maid. Aleric is ageing; his hair greys at the temples and lines cover his face but he is still strong and proud. Germin wonders how long his sister will be safe with the general now; she must also be bearing the scars of age and, surely, he will look elsewhere soon. Then he must be ready to act; he cannot let her life end. That is the only way he can ever repay her. That, and watching the child of her closest friend become a man.

"Germin." Baelar is in front of him. "Do I have to go to the academy?"

"Yes." Germin nods. "We all do. You can learn no more here."

Baelar sighs and stares out of the window into

the marbled square. Others like him are gathering.

"Then let us go." He takes a deep breath. "Will I see you again?"

"Why of course," Germin laughs. "We will still be boarding in the same barracks. I will never be far away."

As they walk into the concourse Germin spies a tall lean figure standing against one of the pillars. He feels a chill run down his spine and without realising places a protective hand on Baelar's back.

"Watch that one." He whispers. "There is talk. He is cruel."

Baelar stares at the figure and has the uneasy sensation of the hidden eyes running over him.

"I'll be fine." He smiles at Germin. "I intend to behave!"

"Good." Germin takes the boy's hand. "Now go and I will find you later."

As he watches the boy take his place Germin tries to fight back the feeling of dread that beats at him. He must be vigilant. No harm can come to the boy now.

As he returns to the barracks Germin sees Aleric waiting at the door.

"He is gone?"

Germin is puzzled.

"Sir? Who? I don't know what you mean."

"Yes, you do. "There is the faintest hint of

Aleric's pale eyes glittering behind his mask. "I have watched you protect that boy since he came from the birthing house. Now you must let him go. His fate is no longer in your hands. Whoever he is, he is no longer yours to worry over."

Germin goes to speak and then hesitates. To say too much would give the situation away. It would reveal to the general that the woman he takes to his bed is Germin's sister and that the boy is the child of her maid. He would need to know how Germin knew of the boy and questions may be asked. Germin was not sure how Aleric would react to the fact that he had also bedded Clara. He had seen them in public many times and if he did not know better; if he did not understand the rules that they lived by, he would swear to the fact that Aleric cared for her; more than a general ever should.

It is three weeks before Germin can speak to Baelar again. Try as he might, he cannot get the boy alone. He finds him one night standing alone in the courtyard of the barracks staring at the full moon that can be seen faintly through the dust.

"Baelar! How has it been?" Germin slaps his back and smiles.

The boy turns to him and Germin hesitates. Here in the barracks, there is no need to hide behind a mask. Each man knows the other. He sees the boy is pale and drawn and lines of worry dance at the edge of his eyes.

"What?" Germin lifts his chin. "What is it?"

"Nothing." Baelar looks at Germin's kindly freckled face and the copper-coloured hair that spikes from his head. "I am just a little tired."

"Hmm. Well in that case you should not be standing out here, you should be asleep."

"Yes." The boy nodded. "I just needed some air that's all."

"Good. Remember if you need anything come and find me. Yes?"

"Yes." Baelar gives a half smile. "I will see you soon Germin."

As he walks away Germin's mind begins to race, he must ask questions and find out what is making the boy troubled so soon in his training.

Miles away in her neat kitchen Elle is busy at the oven. She loves to cook and enjoys the smell of baking that fills the house. Clara sits at the table watching her.

"So" She hesitates, not sure how much of the information Aleric gives her that she should pass on. "So, Baelar has moved into the Academy. Aleric saw him enter."

"Already?" Elle turns her face stricken. "He is so young!"

"He is twelve years now; all boys enter at twelve then at sixteen they have the parade so that they can become soldiers."

"Too young." Elle rubs at her face with flour covered hands. "He should be playing in the dirt, riding ponies, chasing sticks with a dog."

"Yes, he should be." Clara pats her arm. "So should every young man born in this place, but they do not. This is their normality. This is all they know."

Elle stares out of the window. It looks towards the mountains. Somewhere, up there, is the village she once called home. She wonders what remains of it. If anything. She can see a line of trucks rolling down the hillside, bringing more women to be showered, shaved, and used in the breeding houses.

"By the gods." She throws the pan of cakes to the floor. "Will it never end? Will there never be enough?"

"No." says a calm voice behind them. "There will always be a need for more."

Aleric stands in the doorway. A downward glance at the scattered cakes sends Elle rushing to clear them. He watches in silence. He is grown thicker around the middle, but the strength of his arms and thighs is still clear.

Clara feels her stomach lurch as it always does when she is with him and instinctively her hands rise to smooth her hair. Behind his mask Aleric's eyes soften and he smiles. He loves the way that she still wants to look good for him. He knows she is ageing, that there are lines about her eyes and mouth, her breasts are not as firm as they once were. But she still has her tumbling glossy mane of hair and sparkling green eyes. She still clings to him in the nights and fills him with passion. He knows that many have hinted it is time to look for another; that people are talking in the Palace corridors, accusing him of having "emotions" for the woman. So, what if he has feelings for her? Clara will stay.

He has no intention of looking elsewhere.

She is enough.

CHAPTER 13

Baelar knows he is waiting. It is the same every day; when Baelar finishes his training and goes to bathe the tall, thin, man watches him. He never removes the black mask that hides his face, even inside the barracks where the men can be free. He reminds Baelar of the insects he sees hiding in the dirt in the courtyard. But insects he can stamp upon, crush beneath the heel of his boot. The man is different. Against him Baelar has no power. He tries every day to avoid the man; leaves with the first group, waits until all the other boys are gone but it is of no use; the man is always there.

At first Baelar believed that he was trying to help him; to be a friend, a mentor in the same way that Germin has been. Despite Germin's warnings of the man's cruelty he had been kind and had given Baelar tips on ways to improve his fitness and cope with the rigours of the training.

And then it had begun.

The touching. Fleeting at first, a caressing touch on his buttocks, a finger roaming freely on his thighs. Then a hand resting on his crotch; a hand that began to clutch at the zip of his leather trousers and reach for what was inside.

At first Baelar was too shocked to speak. Then when he had found his voice, he had received a beating. Baelar knows what the man wants now; he knows why he waits; he knows what will happen if he resists. He knows that if he fights him the beating that follows will be far worse than the act that follows. So, he no longer fights, no longer resists. It is better to submit and pray that it will be over quickly.

Baelar sits in the bathing rooms and watches the other boy's dress. He knows the man, whose name he now knows to be Officer Lichen, will wait as long as he needs to. He could rush to dress and catch up with the other boys but there would be a pretence, a reason for him to be called back. Better to remain seated and when Lichen comes to him submit to his demands. He is staring at the floor, waiting for the now familiar voice when the door opens and Germin walks in.

The relief Baelar feels is immense and he gets to his feet and smiles broadly as his friend comes over to him. Germin carries his metal mask in his hand. His red hair is spiked with sweat and his face is flushed.

"Baelar." He shakes his head as the boy salutes him. "No need to salute me. How goes it with you?"

"Well." Baelar hesitates. "The training is hard, but I am okay with it. I am just a little tired."

Germin looks at the boy, sees the shadows below his eyes and then spies the bruises on his shoulders. There are marks on his back that appear to have been made by teeth.

"What are these?" The boy flinches as he touches them.

"The boys play a little rough." Baelar turns away hastily and reaches for his undershirt. "It is nothing."

"You should take more care; a wound like that can become easily infected."

"Yes." Baelar reaches for his trousers. "I will, thank you."

Germin watches as the boy salutes him again and walks towards the door, as he does so a tall dark figure steps out of the shadows and starts to follow him.

Germin frowns.

Keeping his distance, always remembering to be out of sight, he walks behind them.

He watches as Lichen takes Baelar into a side room and closes the door; he can hear voices, and then sounds of muffled moans. The hairs rise on the back of Germin's neck, and he feels anger course through his veins. He had heard the tales of Lichen's cruelty to the young trainees; sessions of punishment that were akin to torture, of whipping, of deprivation, but this makes him uneasy. This is different. This breaks the codes by which they all live.

Germin stays where he is, hidden, until the door reopens and Baelar emerges. There is a shadow on his face that tugs at Germin's heart.

He lets the boy go; now is not the time. He waits until Lichen has left the room and then shadows him, forever keeping his distance until they are out into the pale light of the courtyard. Lichen walks quickly and re-enters the training rooms. Germin is about to follow him and then hesitates; he needs to watch him and gather evidence. A few muffled sounds from behind a closed door will not be proof of anything. But one thing he is sure of. This will stop; it is time that Lichen's reign of cruelty comes to an end.

Officer Lichen has been in the barracks for thirty years. He remembers no other home. His room is sparse, bare, devoid of any personality. He has dark olive skin and black eyes. His body is long and lean, hard, and toned with muscle. He looks in the mirror and loosens the knot of hair at the back of his head. His black hair falls straight to his shoulders.

Another secret he keeps hidden from the gold-faced generals.

When he visits the breeding houses the women know they need have no fear of bearing a child. They know that Lichen is there only because it is what is expected of him. Lichen finds no reason to find arousal in the presence of women. If something has stirred in him before he arrives then the act that is carried out is different. No child will ever be born. The women suffer this act reluctantly, but they take comfort in the knowledge that their belly will not swell, and they will be spared the dangers of childbirth. Many of the women Lichen chooses are older. They take no insult in the fact that he finds their female anatomy repulsive and let him take whatever pleasure he can find with resignation. Then, these older women do something that is not normally expected of them.

They listen.

They listen as the strange man in his black mask talks of the boys in his care.

There have been many down the years. Some have fallen deep into his trap and continued the ways that he has taught them into their own adulthood. They are a secret hidden deep from the eyes of the governors and generals. These men and others like them would meet in private to discuss pleasures that only they could understand. Sometimes one would bring a boy for the others to enjoy. Some of the boys had grown and become part of their group; some would not survive and would break. The job would always fall to Lichen to dispose of them when they no longer had a purpose, when their minds were too damaged or when the words that may leave their mouths would endanger the group. It has grown in recent years and more and more men have joined these gatherings. Now they need a larger place to meet, and one boy is not enough.

Lichen has often thought that he would take Baelar to one such gathering. In time. But for now, he prefers to keep the pleasures of the young boy to himself. He fears that the demands of the group will be too much for the boy and he will be the next to break. He does not want to dispose of this one. Not yet.

Raising a leather clad hand, he pulls his hair back into the tight knot at the nape of his neck. He replaces his mask and walks out of the room.

"Officer Lichen." A voice brings him to a halt.

"May I walk with you a while?"

"Officer Germin." Lichen hesitates. "What brings you to the training rooms. How can I help you?"

"There is a boy in your care." Germin falls into step with him. "Baelar is his name. I wondered how he was faring?"

"Baelar? There are many boys in my care, I am afraid I don't recall that name."

Germin is watching the man. Although he cannot see his face, he can clearly see the tension in the muscles of his neck.

"It must be very hard to remember them all, I understand. But this boy is special."

"Special you say?"

"Yes. He has a way with him. A strength. He is very tall with hair the colour of wet earth."

"Ah," Lichen nods. "I think I know the one. Hazel eyes? A strong face?"

"Yes. He will be a handsome man one day."

"Very handsome," Lichen nods and Germin can just make out the silhouette of his tongue darting between his teeth. He feels revulsion churn in his stomach.

"A fine boy," Lichen quickens pace. "He will do well."

"Indeed." Germin lays a hand on Lichen's shoulder and allows his fingers to massage the taut muscles. He must play the game, for now. "I think he will serve the purpose well."

"Ah." Lichen hesitates. He hears the intonation in Germin's voice, but he cannot be sure. "I am not sure what you mean. All the boys in my care are special and make good soldiers."

"Yes." Germin's fingers increase their pressure. "But some have a greater purpose don't you think?"

"Oh." There it was. The understanding. "They do indeed. I did not know you had interest in such things, Germin?"

"It is new to me." Germin steps back and drops his hand. "Some truth I have just discovered in myself."

"Then I shall introduce you to the others."

"Thank you." Germin turns away.

"I will let you know the time and place." Lichen calls after him. "Then you can join us. Your discretion is assured of course."

"Of course." Germin half bows and walks away.

His mind is racing. What should he do? Should he take his suspicions to Aleric? He has no proof. If he gains the proof, will it be too late for Baelar? He must protect him; he has promised Elle. He owes it to Clara. Would Aleric even believe him? Who knows what dark secrets the general keeps to his own counsel.

No. He must continue to play the game. He must discover who else is involved in Lichen's group of unnatural men. He must have enough proof to show the governors that his suspicions are true.

Whoever he takes down when he does so.

CHAPTER 14

Elle walks past the fountain. The gate into the barracks is to her right and looks into a paved courtyard. She stops when she sees them. Young men parading in face masks and leather. Rows of them, some tall, some short some already starting to broaden, some as lean as the branches of a young tree. One of them is her son; her child, her Baelar. But she does not know which one.

The thought rips at her, digging deep inside her chest; a pain greater than any she has yet experienced. It is far, far worse than the act of birthing itself. Her baby, the child she had held in her arms and nurtured at her breast was a stranger to her. Tears prick at her eyes, and she stands at the gate, her hands clutching at the bars.

A man clad in black leather is putting the boys through their exercises. She watches as he moves along the line, a touch here, a pat there, an angry word to some, a kind gesture to others. He returns to one boy far more than the rest. Elle sees him stand behind the boy and pull his shoulders back into an upright position. As he does so the man in black stands close and presses himself against the boys' buttocks.

Elle shudders.

What kind of man is this? This is a new level of depravity she did not know existed. As she walks away, she thinks of Baelar and prays that he has no contact with that man.

From the far side of the courtyard Germin can see her. Sees her hands clutching at the bars. The pain etched on her face. He knows she cannot recognise her son and is glad. He has stayed away from her the past few weeks terrified that his voice will betray his concerns. He stares up at the mountains and tries hard to remember the tiny village where he had once been a boy himself. Sometimes, he can recall walking the paths with his small, scruffy dog, the streets full of the smell of food cooking; and Clara with her tangled red-hair, dirty faced and chiding him.

Guilt and misery make him retch.

What would he give to be that child again playing in the dirt, a barefoot urchin without a care? Free of the trappings of the army and the ruling of this city, the constant striving for control. But he could never be that again, his destiny was set. This is the life he must lead now.

His eyes turn back to Baelar.

Germin has no doubt that his purpose in that life now is to protect the boy.

Clara is sitting in the garden when Elle returns. One look at the expression on her friends face and she can see she is troubled.

"What is it?" She beckons Elle to sit beside her.

"I saw the boys training." Elle places her basket at her feet. "Boys. One of them may have been Baelar. I will never know. I will never see him again."

A tear slides down her cheek.

"Oh Elle!" Clara takes her hand. "I know. I know how hard it is."

'You know?" Elle shakes her head. "How can you know? You are childless. How can you begin to understand?"

Clara gets to her feet and pushes her friend away from her.

"And how would you know what it is to be childless? To never feel the warmth of new life at your breast? To be incomplete; half a woman. A shell, a decoration?"

Elle sees the longing etched all over Clara's face and her heart wrenches with pity.

"I'm sorry. I am sorry Clara. What a cruel hand fate has dealt us."

Clara nods grimly. "But your cards do not spell death. When Aleric tires of me my life is done."

Elle reaches for her and pulls her tight against her.

"Then we must pray that he never does. Come. I bought new lotions at the market today. Let me draw you a bath and make sure that your beauty does not fade."

Clara laughs.

"There are not enough lotions in the world to delay age. That comes to us all."

"But we can make it come more slowly. We have to make sure that Aleric does not tire of your beauty."

CHAPTER 15

Aleric stands at the head of a long narrow table. The wood, a relic of an age long past, is polished so highly that he can see his own reflection. He is troubled. The faces of the governors are all watching him, waiting for a reaction. None of the men in the room wear masks. They are all aged; white haired, with skin that is lined and sallow. These are the leaders who created an army great enough to rule planet. The men who dictate how the population lives its life, who control the future of every child born in every city. These are the men who decide how the lesser mortals die. Men that are not many years from the tombs themselves.

Governor Ratzka is speaking. Aleric forces himself to listen.

"We would like you to consider our offer carefully General Aleric. Join us on the council. Put aside your army days and help us govern. We need a man who can lead in the ways that we have started. A man we can trust. That man is you."

Aleric hesitates. This would be a great honour. But is he ready to leave his men and sit at a table and debate? Is he ready to change the life he has made not only for himself but for Clara? Hidden from the prying eyes of the inner city; safe from those who would observe the emotion that flows between them. To bring her here to the corridors and rooms of the old Palace would mean the end of that privacy. They would be expected to entertain, to play host to the other governors and their companions. She would be forced to spend her life in the society that surrounded the Palace and not spend her time with Elle from whom she gained such comfort. He knows also that here he will be put under pressure, pressure to find a younger woman to share his bed and put his beautiful flame haired Clara aside. That, above all else, he cannot do.

"Thank you for the invitation." He hesitates. "In time I will gladly take my place beside you. But for now, there is still much for me to do to maintain order."

"Oh, come now Aleric." Ratzka laughs. "What is there to do? We control every patch of habitable land, every major city on this planet. What more can we achieve? We just need to make sure that our laws continue."

"I agree." Aleric nods. "And one day I will gladly take on that task. But there are still villages in the hills around this very city that need to be controlled. There can be no long-term stability for our cause while this threat exists."

"Threat?" Ratzka nods. "I know that these villages and the rebels within the hills exist but are they a threat? If they are then surely instant obliteration is the answer?"

"No." A bald headed man with pendulous lips and a paunch sits at the far end of the table. "These villages are where the young girls are about to blossom. If we obliterate, we need to remove all the ripe fruit first."

There is a murmur of agreement amongst the men.

"What do you say, Aleric?" Ratzka narrows his eyes. "Purge these villages of all women both young and old? But if we do this there will surely be no harvest for the future? You believe there are also men in these villages?"

"I do indeed." Aleric nods. "Rebels who hide out in the hills still need somewhere to gather food, and comfort. There are men who evaded capture as children, perhaps hidden well by their mothers or capable of extreme cunning. But a few remain."

"And what can a few men do against the might of the Organisation?"

"One village supports another. As in a barrel of fruit the rot will spread."

"But still Aleric they are no match for us. What weapons do they have?"

"I agree they are no match for us in the way of power. But if word of their resistance grows then soon all the other cities will have the same problem. This band of rebels, however small, needs to be controlled; and swiftly."

"As always, General, you are correct." Ratzka nods. "So, when you have rid our area of these vermin you will come and join us at the table of Council?"

"When there is no more rebellion, yes, I will. But now the threat is too close to these walls to be left unattended."

"Very well." Ratzka gets to his feet. He is small and strikes an unimposing figure beside the soldier. "Do your duty Aleric. When you are happy, we will talk again."

Before Aleric can replace his mask the door bursts open and a palace courtesan rushes in.

"General. Governor. Please excuse the intrusion but General Aleric is needed in the lower city. There is trouble."

"Trouble?" Aleric clips his mask over his face and reaches for his jacket.

"I do not know of what sort, sir. All I know is I was asked to call you urgently."

Aleric nods his farewells to the Council and follows the courtesan. At the door of the Palace an officer is waiting.

"General." His head bows in deference. "The lower city. There is report of some disturbance."

"Of what kind." Aleric climbs into the vehicle.

"An unlawful activity is taking place; the residents are unhappy and there is danger of trouble."

"Unlawful? In what way is it unlawful?" Aleric grips his seat as the officer races through the streets.

"I think it is best if you discover for yourself. Sir."

Aleric looks out of the window and frowns. The lower city is home to the lesser ranking citizens of the city. Those who keep the city operating but carrying out the menial tasks. The people there are poor and afraid of the men in masks. They know all too well the penalties they will face if they break the law. Whoever is doing this is either a desperate man or someone from outside the lower city itself without fear of retribution. But whoever they are, the end result will be the same.

The penalty for breaking any law is always death.

CHAPTER 16

Germin walks some way behind Lichen as they make their way through a long narrow alleyway. There are no lights. When they reach the end of the alley Lichen raises the long cane he always carries and raps at a heavy wooden door. One, two, three. A pause and one more sharp rap. The door swings open and they enter.

The room is full, wall to wall with men. Men of all ranks; officers, ranking soldiers and even figures that Germin knows to be members of the Governor's Palace. To one side he sees the purple robes of a member of the Great Council. In the middle of the room is a podium, almost a stage surrounded by ropes. In its centre is a bench made of wood and on the floor is what looks to be a long-lashed whip. Germin feels uneasiness creep into his stomach making it churn and tense.

"Keep your mask on." Lichen mutters. "Do not let anyone see who you are. Never speak your name."

Germin steps back and allows the shadows to swallow him. He stays close to the wall and watches as Lichen walks away. Sweat is dampening his palms and wetting the back of his neck, he feels it begin to trickle down his spine. He had not expected something of this scale, or this atmosphere of dark intent filling the air. A tension is rippling through the crowd. A door at the far side of the stage opens and a man wearing the uniform of a palace guard walks in. Behind him is a boy. Tall, dark, lean, and pale with a face dominated by terrified eyes. They dart around the room looking for sanctuary, finding none. He wears a mask over his lower face but as he reaches the middle of the stage the guard pulls it from him.

The boy drops his head.

The guard lifts it roughly with his hand and nods to two waiting attendants. Germin can see the anguish on the boy's face as his clothes are removed until he stands naked in front of a crowd of jostling excited men. The palace guard turns him so that he can be seen by all sides of the room. Germin can see marks on the boy's back. Marks made by a whip. Then the guard steps back and nods. There is a surge amongst the audience and a tide of bodies press forward. The boy disappears, briefly, and then Germin can see clearly what is happening.

Germin tastes bile in his throat as he watches man after man mount the stage, He must get out of here, away from this crowd of sick, perverse, cheering men. He begins to fight his way back to the door and as he reaches it, he realises the crowd has become silent. He glances over his shoulder and sees that the boy is gone, and Lichen is walking up the steps into the middle of the room. Fear grips Germin and he feels his head spin.

Walking behind Lichen, head bowed, shoulders slumped is Baelar. Even with the mask that covers his mouth Germin knows him. He freezes, unable to move, unable to breathe, his heart pumps loudly in his chest and adrenalin surges through his veins. He stands and watches in horror as Baelar is stripped naked and displayed to the crowd. Lichen is proud of his presentation and in a macabre display of control begins to flick the whip across Baelar's thighs, making him flinch and recoil. Then he steps back and offers the whip to the men who are pressing forward.

Two men mount the stage first. One sits on the bench, takes Baelar's hands and pulls him onto his knees, the other moves around the stage and stands behind him. His mouth breaks into a wide, sadistic grin and with a flourish he removes his own robes. He braces himself and raises his arm, whip in hand, high above his own head. His eyes run around the room as he taints his audience, as they watch in anticipation.

His arm begins to swing downward, and as it does a flash of steel dances across his throat.

Blood spurts downward over Baelar's back. There is a thud and the body, drained quickly of life, falls to the floor beside them. Germin stands back and lowers his blade. Spots of blood drip onto his boots. He can feel the eyes of the crowd upon him, Lichen is moving forward, cane raised to strike. A rage takes over Germin that removes any of his remaining restraint and gives him strength. His blade glints as he thrusts and stabs at the men who approach him. One after another they succumb to his fury; he begins to revel in the feeling of his knife cutting into their flesh, hearing their cries as they fall. Baelar is shuddering at his feet, covered in the blood of the bodies that are strewn beside him. In the distance Germin sees a long lean figure fleeing the carnage and making for a side door. This cannot happen. Lichen knows who he is and will reveal him to save his own skin. Germin grabs Baelar by the arm and pulls him to his feet.

"Come on." He begins to drag him through the crowd, his fury and flashing knife cutting a swathe through all who would block his path. Baelar staggers behind him wearing only a red cloak of blood. They reach the door and looking back Germin sees that the men are crushing towards the main exit; the stench of blood and fear surrounds him. He snatches an overcoat that is draped over a chair. He throws it over Baelar's shoulders and pushes him outside.

"Run!" He tells him. "Get out of here! I will come and find you. Stay hidden."

Germin knows which route Lichen will take, the one that they had walked less than an hour previously, and he races swiftly through the dark alleys retracing his steps. He sees him. Barely a shadow as he moves from doorway to doorway, keeping himself hidden. Germin slows to a walk and begins to stalk him silently, the trained hunter is tracking down his enemy.

Softly. Quietly. Waiting for the moment to arrive.

It does so as Lichen turns towards another street and creeps out of the shadow of the buildings. Before he has taken two steps an arm closes around his neck and brings him to his knees.

Lichen gasps and tries to regain his feet but the arm that holds him is powerful. He looks up, his breathing heavy, and for a second feels terror as he looks at the black figure bending over him. There is a sharp pain, heat sears through his chest and his head begins to spin. Then a comforting wave of lightheaded peace floods through him as he drops to the floor.

Germin watches him fall and lowers his blade. He takes a deep breath. It is done.

Then a blow catches him from behind and sends him reeling toward the ground; a strong hand grasps his shoulder and hauls him back to his feet. He turns his head; and looks straight into the expressionless metal face of General Aleric.

CHAPTER 17

Germin sits in the dark cellar and stares at the wall. He wears no mask now. There is no need to hide his identity here in this cell; nor will there be when he leaves it. His palms are damp with sweat, but he is cold, always cold. Gone is his leather uniform; he wears trousers and a shirt of coarse cloth. He is no longer part of the great army, no longer part of the machine that maintains control. He is just Germin. The man who was once a boy that failed in his attempt to hide from the men in masks.

He sobs.

If he closes his eyes, he can still smell the iron tang of the blood, the acrid undertone of fear that had filled the room that night. He can feel the blade in his hand penetrating the flesh beneath it; feel the adrenaline coursing through his veins and look through the redness that had filled his mind. He had been trained to kill and kill, he had. His masked face had been the last image Lichen saw, and he had known who had brought about his end. The man he had been duped into believing shared the same unnatural perverse interests as him.

Germin shudders.

His mind turns to Baelar. Where is he? Has he returned to the barracks or is he still hiding in the lower city. Waiting for Germin to fill his promise; a promise he would no longer be able to keep. He thinks of Elle and is glad that she is unaware of her son's plight. Then he thinks of Clara. His sister's face and bouncing red curls swim before his eyes. She will attend the execution. She will see him.

She will know his fate.

He knows what that fate will be. Death is the only answer, he understands the laws of the Council. What will she feel, he thinks, when she sees him die? Will she cry tears of sorrow or feel relief that he is gone? She will never know how his actions have haunted him, the regret, the pain every time he thinks about what happened between them. His chance to say he is sorry has gone. She will never know what he has done to try and make amends. His vow to never let her end come before its natural time; his promise to Elle, his watching of Baelar who is now the closest he will ever come to having a relationship with a son of his own. Even in that he has failed. Perhaps it is best that his wretched life will soon be over. He shudders and places his face in his hands where tears run silent through his fingers.

The door creaks and grinds open. Germin leaps to his feet in a single bound, his heart pounding in his chest.

Is it to be now? So soon?

Aleric stands in the doorway.

"Relax." He commands. "It is not time."

Germin sinks back onto the bed and waits for his panic to subside. He tastes bile in his throat and heaves. When he speaks, his voice, unused for the last few days is little more than a whisper.

"The boy. Baelar. Have you found him?"

"No." Aleric shakes his head. "So far there is no trace. That is why I am here. Do you have any idea where he may be hiding?"

"No. I told him to wait for me and I would find him. I hoped he would have gone back to the barracks."

"He doesn't know Lichen is dead. Why would he return there?"

"Then he must be in the lower city somewhere. Please Aleric, sir, I know what my fate will be, but he is just a boy. Please find him and make sure he is safe."

"It is my duty to keep all of my soldiers safe, including those still in the Academy." Aleric snorts. "I will do my best to locate the boy. But tell me Germin, why is this boy so important to you? What made you act in the way that you did?"

"I made a promise to his mother that I would watch over him. I failed. I had to put it right."

"His mother?" Aleric frowns. "How did this happen? Are you the boy's father?"

"No." Despite his situation Germin is forced to laugh. "You think with hair like mine I am that boy's sire? No, I do not know who sired him. I was on duty the day they took him from her, so I made her a promise. A promise that has brought me to my end."

"It is a strange promise for a soldier to make to some wretch in the breeding houses."

"I know her. Or I did once. Before I was brought here to the city."

"You remembered her? That is impossible, you were a child."

"No, it was she who remembered me." Germin hesitates, and tries to slow his thoughts, he is stepping onto treacherous ground.

"So many women here yet you happen upon one who remembers you. In the breeding houses? How did she see you?"

"No." Germin shakes his head and feels his nerves tingle, he has already said too much. "She heard my name is all."

"How? Where was she, this woman, to recognise you?"

"She was with the child in the courtyard; she heard my name. After they took the boy, I promised to watch over him; she was in such despair. Then she was taken from the breeding houses. She became a maid."

"A maid?" Aleric is still. "How do you know this? How do you know she is a maid?"

"She is your maid!" The rope of tension inside him snaps and Germin jumps to his feet. "Yours. Her name is Elle. The boy is hers."

Aleric stands close to Germin.

"My maid, Elle?"

Germin stares at him, pale green eyes glittering in the half light.

"Yes."

For a fleeting second, he reminds Aleric of someone else.

Germin sits again. He feels weak. He has said too much and hovers too near the truth.

"How can she remember you? You were a boy. Nothing but a boy when you were brought here, and you wear a mask as a man."

"My name, as I told you. She heard my name, that is all. It was a name often used in our family. We were children together."

How smoothly and easily the lies pass his lips. It is too late for him now, but he must make sure that the others come to no harm.

"At first, I couldn't remember my home; but the more she spoke of it the more I remembered. Memories came back of games played in the dirt. Her voice, her eyes, made me think of that time when I was a child."

Aleric stares at the dark red hair on Germin's head. Thoughts are brewing inside him that he fights hard to suppress.

"Do many from your village have hair as red as yours?"

"How do I remember? As you said, I was a boy. But I think it's likely. You see them now when they bring the women from the villages. They all look similar. Some villages are dark skinned, some are fair. The colour runs within them."

"Indeed. But red hair is not common."

"You know what villages are like General Aleric. One family breed with another. Sometimes even father with daughter. The genes spread quickly."

Aleric nods, Germin speaks the truth.

"Aleric. Sir?" Germin looks up.

"Don't let Elle come to the execution. She must not know I am dead, and she must never know what has happened to her son."

Aleric nods.

"On that you have my word. But I will not stop trying to find him; I will make sure his name and yours are removed from all public details of the trial."

"Trial? Why must there be a trial? We both know I am to die. Can you not save me from the anguish and run me through now?"

"I cannot do that. But one thing I do promise you. I will make sure the end comes swiftly."

"Thank you." Germin's voice breaks. "That is all I can ask for."

"With regret, Germin, I agree."

CHAPTER 18

Clara lays her head upon Aleric's broad shoulder and runs her finger down his jaw. He is staring at the ceiling with troubled eyes.

"What is it?" She snuggles into him. "That can make you so far from me?"

Aleric turns his head and looks at her. He wants nothing more than to unload this burden onto her. To tell her what had happened only a few short nights ago. It has played on his mind ever since; the scene in that dreadful place; the knowledge of what had taken place there. The carnage, the bodies, and the realisation that one of his own men had taken the law into his own hands and killed other soldiers and members of the Palace. What troubles him deeply is the knowledge that he understands why Germin has done this. He understands the disgust, the compassion for the boy. But he is a general. He has to put such thoughts aside and carry out the letter of the law. He must be what he is trained to be, a soldier. The judging of the crime will fall to the Council, but he knows what the punishment will be, they will just decide how it is to be carried out. He sighs deeply and closes his eyes. To unburden himself would be a great relief. But in doing so he would have to impart the worst knowledge of all; that Elle's son had been one of the victims and that currently they could find no trace of the boy.

"Please Aleric." Clara kisses his cheek. "Share some of your troubles. I hate to see you like this."

Aleric opens his eyes and lets them roam over her face. She is so warm and trusting. He lifts a hand and lets it trace the curves of her body. This is natural. Not what Lichen and those other sick creatures did with the boys. It sickens him and fills him with rage.

"It is too difficult to explain." He closes his eyes again so that she cannot see the torment in them. "Just lie with me and be peaceful, that is all I need."

"If only it was that simple." Clara kisses his arm. "But I know you well now, and that will not be enough."

"No. You are right." Aleric sits up, suddenly, and causes the sheets to fall from their naked bodies. "But if I tell you?"

"What?" Clara sits up and places her arms around him. "What do you think will happen? Who will I tell? The birds, the trees, the flowers in the garden?"

"Elle." He says simply. "You will tell Elle. You tell her everything. But this Clara runs deeper than idle gossip."

"I promise." She pulls him round to face her. "I will tell no one not even Elle. Anyway, you know you have the power to silence me."

Aleric shakes his head.

"I pray that day will never come."

"One day it will. It must. If I am still alive and you should die before me, I will have no use, or you will tire of me before then. But it will happen."

"No." Aleric takes her face in his hands. "I hope and pray that when you leave this life it will be at the right time and with me beside you. Life without you is unbearable to think of."

"Not what a general should say." Clara teases.

"No, it is not. But it is what I wish for. If it will happen is not for us to decide or to think about."

"So will you tell me?"

Aleric breathes deeply. He needs to unburden his mind. To someone not driven and controlled by the ways of the Council.

"There was some trouble in the Lower City. Men, including soldiers, all gathered for the sake of taking pleasure with young boys."

Clara shakes her head.

"Is that not against the law?"

"It is. But some men believe they are above the law. I was called to stop the residents of the Lower City causing a riot. They knew what was

133

happening and wanted it stopped. When I entered the building with my men there was chaos. Men were running in all directions and there were bodies laid on the floor."

"The citizens did this?"

"No. At first, I could not see who the cause of the deaths was, then I saw two figures running. I caught up with them as one killed the other. A soldier, one of my men, taking the life of one of the barrack instructors. I was too late to prevent it."

"If the instructor was one of the men who took pleasure in young boys, then why would you want to stop it?"

"Because it is not for me to hand out justice based on my own thoughts. There is a process that needs to be followed. But it does not mean that I would not wish those men dead myself."

"So, what will happen now?"

"The man will stand trial. To what end I don't understand as we already know what the penalty will be. What the trial will decide is how and where. I fear a public spectacle will need to be made."

"That is sad. To have to die for stopping something that is wrong."

"Indeed. But he should have come to me. He should have trusted I would have acted on his words."

"And would you?"

"Of course!"

"Perhaps he was afraid you would not believe him." Clara lies back down and pulls the sheets over herself.

"Perhaps. Now it is too late for him. His remaining days will be short."

Clara watches him as he lays down beside her. Her mind races through what she has been told. She thinks of the boys, the men who have died and the man who is yet to die. She feels anger, disgust but most of all she feels pity. For both the condemned man and the man beside her.

CHAPTER 19

Baelar watches the door that leads into the confinement quarters of the barracks. On his back are the plain brown clothes of a tradesman, stolen from the laundry room of a house in the lower city. In his hand is a sack of provisions. Taking a deep breath, he walks to the door. The guard watches him, eyes moving behind his mask.

"What have you there boy?"

"Provisions." Baelar opens the sack. "Fruit, and vegetables."

"Ah." The soldier reaches into the sack and pulls out a piece of ripe fruit. "Late, aren't you? Still, on you go. You know where the kitchen is."

"Of course." Baelar nods and half bows. "Thank you, Sir."

Once inside the building Baelar stays close to the wall, letting the dim lighting cover his movements. He has no idea which room Germin is held in, but he intends to find out. He knows he is here; he has heard the talk in the lower city. What he can do by finding him he doesn't know, but he has to try. The corridor is long and lined with doors. Each one is sealed with a small window that can slide open. Some feet ahead one of the doors opens, and light floods into the narrow walkway. Baelar breathes in sharply and presses himself close to the wall, head bowed. The tall, imposing, figure of General Aleric is stepping out of the room. Quickly Baelar bends down and busies himself with the contents of his sack. The general, gold mask gleaming dully in the half-light walks straight past. A shiver runs over Baelar's skin. There is something about the general; his broad shoulders, the way his powerful muscles move beneath the leather uniform, the imposing stride, which makes him nervous. There goes a man that has the power of an army at his command, a man with the life or death of others at his fingertips. General Aleric is very much a man to be feared.

Baelar steadies his nerves and looks back to the door that the general has come out of. He knows, without question, that Germin is in the room behind the door. Why else would the great general have been here? He reaches the door and tugs open the small window hatch. In the gloom he sees a motionless figure.

"Germin!" He hisses. "Germin, is that you?"

The face that appears before him is pale, filled with clear green eyes and topped by copper hair darkened with sweat.

"Baelar!" Germin reaches through the bars and

grasps his hand. "Baelar! You are safe!"

"Yes." Baelar clutches at the bars with his free hand. "But you? What has happened? I have to get you out of here!"

"No Baelar. There is only one route open to me now. That route does not include life."

"No!" Tears spring into Baelar's eyes and make their way slowly down his dirty cheeks.

"No, they cannot do this. You were protecting me, you were trying to save me, to save all of us from those men. I will go to them and tell them what it was like!"

"They already know." Germin shakes his head. "But they must uphold the law. It is forbidden to take the life of another without a decree from the Great Council."

"What they did to us is a crime! Torture is a crime! Surely, they can see that if you had not killed those men then they would have been sentenced to death anyway?"

"Baelar. It is the law, we know this."

"Then it's wrong." Baelar snatches his hand free. "I must get you out of here. I must. But how?"

"You can't," Germin can see the boy's anguish, his own pain reflected in the tear-filled eyes. "Promise me that you won't try. You must stay safe."

"I will not go back there and become one of them!"

"Baelar, they will keep looking for you. It is better to go to them now and come to no harm."

"No. I have heard talk in the Lower City. Outside this city there are villages, people still live in these villages."

"I know." Germin sighs heavily. "I was a boy in such a place."

"There are men there, men who hide away in the hills and plan the downfall of the army. Men who want to rid the world of metal masks and the monsters that wear them. I will go to them. They will help me."

"Baelar, no. Do not do this. You will be caught, and you will share my fate. I cannot let that happen. I promised her I would keep you safe!"

"Promised who?"

"Someone who cared for you as a baby." Germin curses his own carelessness." I was there the day they took you. I promised I would watch over you."

"My mother?" Baelar's voice is barely a whisper.

"Just a woman who cared for you as a child. That is all."

Baelar stares at the man in front of him. None of the boys in the training camp knew who had sired or birthed them. In truth it was not something they ever thought about for too long. They were there to be soldiers; where they came from had no part in the great plan that charged their lives. But in the few days he had hidden in the Lower City he had seen women properly for the first time. Women working, carrying out the menial tasks that were needed to keep the organisation alive. He had seen them walking and talking and had seen how they looked at him. It was one such woman who had offered him food and a bed in the store house. She saw him for what he was, not a soldier in the making but a boy; a boy who was lost and confused. He suppresses a pang of guilt that the clothes he wears were stolen from the same storehouse.

It had also been in the streets of the Lower City that he had heard of the Breeding Houses and the acts that the soldiers carried out there. For the first time in his life Baelar had wondered about the woman who had birthed him and what may have happened to her.

"I am going to the village." Baelar looks up. "I don't care about the risk. There is no place here for me now. I have no wish to be part of this army that will kill one man because he protects another!"

"Baelar. Please." Germin rubs at his eyes with his dirty, still bloodstained hands. "If they catch you, you will die alongside me."

"Then we will be together." Baelar turns and is walking away. "I will do this for you Germin, even if I do die trying."

CHAPTER 20

The dawn is just beginning to break through the misty sky. A pale light begins to fill the ramshackle streets of the Lower City. As the light increases so life begins to emerge. From the corner where he sits, hood pulled hard forward to hide his face, Baelar watches and waits. He knows who he is waiting for. The man the people call Jarel, who arrives each day with the truck that brings provisions from the villages into the city. Each morning, he unloads his wares in the same place and then goes back into the hills to collect the next day's load. There will be a time, albeit short, when he goes to eat, and his truck stands unguarded. That is when Baelar will act. He sits without movement as the truck pulls into place and Jarel carries sack after sack into the storehouse. Then, when the man enters the ncighbouring Inn to eat, he moves, light footed and swift. He climbs through the door into the back of the truck. On the floor are empty sacks, covering himself from head to toe he hides beneath them.

He lies there for what feels to his nervous mind

an age and then he hears voices. The door to the cab of the truck slams shut, the engine fires up and the truck begins to move. Instantly Baelar feels a chill rush over him. Cold air is flowing through the vehicle to keep its contents fresh on their journey. Baelar scrabbles for more sacks and huddles beneath them, struggling to keep warm.

The truck rumbles on. In the cold, dark, space Baelar has no idea of how far they have travelled or how long it will take to reach the gates of the city. The vehicle comes abruptly to a halt. He holds his breath and listens carefully. Suddenly the door swings open and a flashlight sweeps around the interior. There is a pause and then the sacks are swept off him, the blinding glare of a flashlight making him curl into a ball.

"Well. What have we got here?"

Baelar peers through his fingers and sees Jarel looking down at him.

Jarel wears no metal mask. A simple cloth is knotted over his nose and around his long, greasy hair. His eyes are black, and his nose protrudes like the beak of a great hunting bird.

"A little stowaway. Get up boy. Who are you? What are you doing in my truck?"

"Please." Baelar scrambles to his feet and nods his head in a bow. "I need to get to the villages."

"The villages? Why? Runaway, are you? Is there a bounty on your head?"

"No. But I need to get away from this place. That is all."

"Why would that be? I know what you are. Trying to run from the barracks?"

"My friend is in danger." Baelar looks at the floor, nervous. "I need to get help."

"Help!" Jarel laughs." What help will you find in the village's boy? Come let me take you back to the barracks, whatever it is you have done I am sure it can be corrected."

"No!" Baelar looks to the door, judging the distance to make his escape. "I will never go back there; I would rather die."

"If they catch you trying to flee then die you will. You think that they don't search these vehicles? That others have not tried to escape before you? This friend of yours, what has he done?"

"He protected me. Other boys also. Now he will die for saving us. I must try and stop it."

Jarel hesitates.

"This friend. Is he a soldier?"

"Yes." Unbidden tears begin to flow from Baelar's eyes. "He is the only friend I have. Please. Please help me."

"Is he the one that took a blade to that monster Lichen?"

"Yes."

143

"You were one of the unfortunates that got taken by him?"

"Yes." Memories flood back into Baelar's mind, and he begins to sob, shoulders heaving up and down as he gasps for breath.

"Easy now." Jarel places an arm on his shoulders. "Calm yourself. I shed no tears for the death of that evil creature or his accomplices. The thought of them makes me sick to my stomach."

"Then will you help me?"

"Against my judgement I will get you out of the city boy if that is what you wish, although I do not see what it will achieve. The man is condemned and there is little that can change that. If they catch you then he will at least have company when he dies. What is it you think you can do to prevent this?"

"I don't know," Baelar shrugs. "But I have to try. There are men in these villages. Perhaps they will help me."

"Look at you!" Jarel laughs. "A boy taking on the might of the army single handed. You have courage, I will give you that. Where did you think you were going in the back of my truck, eh?"

"To the nearest village."

"Without being caught? Without being discovered when they search the vehicle? Brave but stupid."

Baelar shrugs. Put into words his plan does seem

foolhardy.

"Even on foot the city wall is guarded constantly. Nothing gets in or out without them knowing."

Feeling suddenly weak, Baelar sits heavily on the floor and places his head in his hands. A wave of sympathy washes over Jarel and he sits beside him.

"Fortunately for you, you chose to stowaway in my truck. I'll not hand you in, boy. That man Lichen was an evil being. There is more than one boy in the streets of the Lower City broken beyond repair because of him and his cohorts. The soldier who killed him deserves a medal not a bullet."

Without warning Baelar feels bile rise in his throat and is violently sick.

"So now I have your mess to clean up as well, eh boy?" Jarel pats him on the back. "Don't worry, that's the anxiety coming out of you, that is all. Now, we have to make sure no one will see you for who you really are."

Within minutes Jarel has produced a gilet of coarse wool and a long heavy brown cloak. He also gives Baelar a face covering the same as his own.

"Now. Put these on, wipe up that mess with the sack there and get in the front, quickly, before someone comes."

Baelar climbs into the front of the vehicle and is grateful for the warmth coming from the engine.

Jarel hands him an identity card.

"When they stop us, which they will, pretend to be asleep. When they rouse you show them this but don't speak. Understand?"

Baelar nods. The card in his hand bears the image of a boy similar in age to himself. A boy not too unlike in colouring and appearance.

"Who is this?"

"My son." The bitterness gives Jarel's voice a rough edge. "He was my o. In the days before they took him."

"Where is he now? He looks of similar age to me, perhaps I know of him?"

"He is dead." Jarel cuts him short. "He never recovered from what Lichen and his band of twisted perverts did to him. Took his own life. Do you know what they called him? The monsters behind the masks? A coward! Not worthy of a soldier's burial. They brought his body back to the village and dumped it in the square clad in rags. He had been gone for a year. One year."

"I am so sorry." Baelar stares at the face in his hands.

"You see boy, I have wished Lichen dead many, many times. The friend you wish to rescue has seen my wishes done. So, I will try and aid you on this fool's errand, I can see no good coming from it mark you, but I will try. No man should face execution for ridding the world of such a low life bastard as Lichen."

Baelar stares out of the window of the truck. He can feel Jarel's pain, but more powerful than that, he can feel the shame and anguish that had tormented the boy in the image to his death. It is the same sickness that has haunted him for many months.

"Now." Jarel pulls the card from his hand. "We are nearly at the gates. Pretend to sleep and remember not to speak."

The hills climb steeply and as they do the temperature drops. Baelar shivers as a draught comes through the door. Jarel's plan of getting past the city guards has worked and having now seen the armed guards, the spotlights, and the giant electrified gates Baelar knows he would never have made the crossing unaided. The whole city wall, Jarel has told him, carries an electric current strong enough to stop a man's heart. The only way in, or out, was past the guarded gates.

He has never really seen the city, only the insides of the Barracks and training yards. He has watched as the tall white buildings gave way to smaller dwellings with gardens and courtyards where fountains danced. He has seen small open spaces and trees. Then, outside the walls he sees the waste; sees mile after mile of burnt earth; the ruined buildings that stand stark against the skyline, only their bare bones remaining. Here and there is the sight of a shrub trying to reach up for the light, craving an existence on the dry ground. But it is a silent landscape where nothing moves. As the vehicle climbs higher Baelar looks down on the city from above. There is the giant circle that houses the Government buildings, the Palace, the dwellings, and roads all ringed by the wall. To the South the courtyards and fountains, to the North the half-broken houses of the Lower City. Baelar wishes Germin could see this. That he could look down from the slow-moving vehicle and see that the might of the Council and its army was contained in that one small space.

Mile after mile they climb until the dawn has long since passed and the chill of early morning begins to fade. They enter a village, a small cluster of stone houses; animals roam freely on the streets and drink water from the trough at the centre of the square. Jarel brings the truck to a halt and with a sigh pulls down his hood and removes his face covering.

Baelar stares.

Jarel has thick black hair that hangs to his shoulder and has something on his face that Baelar has never seen before. A beard.

"Stay here." He gets out of the vehicle. "I will get us something to eat and to drink. We will not stop here, the place we need is further into the hills. Stay inside, many here work closely with the army."

Baelar sits back and closes his eyes. He has no desire to get out and stand exposed in this strange place. Weariness rises in him like a tide and long before Jarel returns he is asleep.

CHAPTER 21

Aleric stands in the courtyard at the rear of the house and stares up at the sky. Tonight, the haze is thinner, and you can see, in the distance, the lights of the stars. When he was a boy, before the bombs and the burning he had lain for hours watching the stars. It was hard to remember a time when he had not been hidden behind his mask, when every step of his waking hours was governed by the needs of the Council. He thinks of the boys growing in the breeding houses, of the young men being trained to carry on the duty he had loyally fulfilled since taking oath many years ago. For a moment he feels pity. Will they ever look at the stars? Behind him he can hear Clara in conversation with Elle. They are sitting on the veranda and Elle is applying some new scented cream to Clara's shoulders. Normally, at this stage of the evening he would have dismissed her so that he could remove the mask from his face; but tonight, guilt swayed him. He had been unable to locate the boy Baelar. In this rare moment of sentiment Aleric imagined the girl's pain should she know her son was lost. So, he left them to their idle chatter a while longer and continued to watch the stars.

"Aleric." Clara calls him. "Aleric come here?"

He swings around and strides over to her. She is holding up a small jar of ointment.

"This is the most wonderful thing. It puts heat into your body, through your skin and soothes the muscles."

"Really?" Aleric takes the jar. "This little thing does all that? We already have medicines that do that Clara."

"But Elle made this." Clara smiles at her friend. "From plants and herbs in our own garden."

"Then I commend your cleverness Elle, and should I have any need of my muscles being warmed I know where to come."

Seeing her friend blush Clara glares at Aleric, anger swelling inside her.

Sensing the awkwardness Elle gets to her feet and quickly gathers up her things.

"I will bid you goodnight, Clara. Sir."

"Why did you do that?" Clara snaps as soon as she is out of earshot. "Why belittle her in that way? What she has made is clever and it works, and we will have no need of meddling physicians prodding and probing us all the time."

"I did not belittle her." Aleric sits beside her. "She is a servant Clara, a maid. I commended her cleverness in making the potion. She is no physician however."

"She is my friend." Clara hisses. "She is the only company I have day after day while you are gone. I want her to feel this is her home."

"She lives here." Aleric looks at her. "It will never be her home."

Clara stares at the expressionless gold mask and sees herself in its reflection. She hates the mask; it hides *him,* hides the Aleric she longs for at night and misses every moment he is away from her.

"Please take that thing off Aleric. I hate it. I want to see you and talk to *you.*"

Aleric looks around him, reluctant to remove his mask outside, but all is quiet. The light is on in Elle's room. He raises his hand and clicks himself free of his mask.

"Is that better?"

"Much." Clara's angst subsides. "What news of the soldier who will stand trial?"

"The trial is set for tomorrow and I expect the execution to be a few days later."

Clara shudders.

"The poor man. To know what your fate is going to be, and that the day is getting closer."

She stops abruptly. Aleric stares at her, knowing the thoughts that were going through her head.

"Clara" He reaches out to her.

"No." She looks away. "Sometimes I am

reminded of what I am to you. Now is one such time."

Her profile is illuminated by the lights behind her. He studies the line of her nose and the defiant lift to her chin. He imagines waking each morning without her beside him. He imagines delivering her to the Medical Unit to be ended.

He shudders.

"You must know what you really are to me. Surely after all these years?" He whispers. "I will always find a way to keep you here. Always."

"Will you?" She does not turn her head. "When you make that final step and join the Council what will you do then? How will you prove to them that they have made the right choice? What will happen when they see that you display emotion; that you are not the great general driven only by ambition they thought you were?"

"You doubt me?"

"Yes, I do." This time she turns. "You are who you are because of *what* you are. Powerful, ruthless, brave: someone that men fear and look up to at the same time. They never see you as I do, and they never will. So, when the time comes you will hide that from them, and however it must happen you will do it."

A breeze drifts across the garden, and it carries the scent of the lotions that Elle has massaged onto her shoulders. His heart quickens.

"Come." He gets to his feet and takes her hand. "Come with me and I will show you what kind of man I am."

Clara looks up at him and sees the light casting shadows on his face. There is a hint of a smile on his lips. She rises slowly and steps forward pressing herself against him, as she does so, he runs his hand down the small of her back and grasps one shapely thigh, pulling it forward over his own.

"It is a pleasant evening." She bites gently at his lip, taunting him. "A shame to waste it."

Aleric looks around him. The house is in silence, all the lights are out; the courtyard is protected by large walls. He grasps at her shoulder and spins her around, pushing her forward over the table. With his free arm he tears her dress and undergarments from her. Clara gasps as the night air caresses her body, a gasp that grows louder as the air is replaced by Aleric's probing hand. As he plunges against her his weight sends them both crashing to the floor and the table spins from beneath them, glasses shattering loudly. Aleric doesn't care. Lifting her hips from the ground he kneels behind her and continues to drive her to release. Clara yelps, pain and pleasure filling her in equal measure, until she collapses forward onto her face as with a great groan he falls to the ground. Through the tangle of her hair, she looks at his motionless figure, his eyes closed and touches his fingers with hers.

A tear slides down her cheek and soaks into the earth of the courtyard. Love was not something that had a place in this life that they led; but it had found its way in.

Elle hears the crash and goes to the window. She stares, transfixed, at the couple below her, at the frantic aggressive love making. She shudders. Anger, revulsion, and pity chase each other through her mind. Then she stops and watches closely as Aleric reaches out to pull Clara to him and wrap her in his arms. Elle watches them for a long time. The couple laying half naked in the dirt, lost to all bar themselves. She can see Aleric's pale hair in the lamplight, the contours of his muscles; can see how strong he is as her eyes roam over his long body and broad shoulders. His face is hidden from her, buried in Clara's flesh. She steps back from the window as Aleric gets slowly to his feet; and lifts Clara with him. Then with a sense of disbelief she sees him kiss her, long and passionate before swooping her up and carrying her into the house.

Elle is confused. Her only contact with men had been the brutality of the breeding houses. She had felt pity for Clara when she had seen them together first; and ever since she had thought her friend as a prisoner making the best of what she had, fulfilling a role she had to play, clinging onto life while she had the chance. But this was something else. This was not just a relationship of lust or necessity.

This was something more.

CHAPTER 22

The figure that stands in front of Baelar is short and slender. Narrow legs in green trousers, face and hair hidden by a black mask and hood. A gun is slung carelessly across their back and a knife glints in a holder at their hip. He can feel them watching him, judging him, looking for signs of weakness.

"So," The figure speaks and with a surprisingly soft voice. "You want us to go into the city, into the lair of those masked murderers and help you to free one of them?"

"Yes. No. He is not one of them. He is different."

"You think we haven't heard this before? Where do you propose we take him? You think there is no risk of them tracking him here?"

"Leave us in the hills. We will find our own way."

The figure laughs and Baelar is confused by the musical tone of the sound.

"I am sure you will. So, what is in it for us?"

"In it?" Baelar is confused.

"What do we get? Money, weapons? What is it to be?"

Baelar hangs his head.

"I have nothing."

"So, you want us to risk our lives to save a mask wearer and you have nothing to give us!"

Jarel steps forward.

"Listen to me. The man the boy wishes to save killed Officer Lichen. He is sentenced to death for ridding the world of a snake."

"Lichen?" A shadow flits across the eyes of the figure. Eyes that are brown and almond shaped with long, thick eyelashes. "Lichen is dead?"

"Yes." Baelar pleads. "My friend killed him for the things he did to me and to others. He was trying to help us. He doesn't deserve to die!"

"On that score I agree." The figure pulls a chair from behind them and sits down; they gesture to Baelar. "Sit. Please. I need to think."

"We don't have time to think." Baelar is growing agitated, time is wasting, every minute they debate is another minute less that Germin has left to live. "We have to reach him before it is too late!"

Jarel moves to the back of the room in which they sit and pulls a heavy curtain across the door.

"Show him." He demands. "Let him know."

The figure hesitates, then, on seeing Jarel's nod, begins to take off their hood and mask.

Baelar stares as the black cloth falls away and reveals the olive-skinned face of a girl.

"You are a girl? Jarel what is this? I was told there were men here who could help me! You bring me to a girl!"

"I can help you." The girl snaps. "But only if you show some respect."

"Sorry." Baelar feels the heat rising to his cheeks and when he speaks his voice is low and embarrassed. "I just don't know what one girl can do against the army."

"There are men here." The girl has a proud and haughty expression. "They listen to me. I am Zora. Jarel here is my father. Lichen is responsible for the death of my brother, and I would like nothing more than to set eyes on the man who killed him and give him my thanks."

"I am so sorry." Baelar hangs his head. "Lichen has ruined many lives it seems."

"But this man. You say he is a friend? Can he be trusted? Will he not go running back with news of our whereabouts hoping for pardon?"

"Zora." Jarel lays a hand on her shoulder "He is condemned to death. He will welcome escape however it comes; there is no fear he will return."

"It won't be easy." Zora looks at him and shakes her head. "There is great risk. But if we succeed it will be a mighty victory for us to free him from the executioner."

Baelar holds his breath. Rivulets of sweat are running down the hollow of his spine. This is his only hope of saving Germin and its fate lies in the hands of one girl.

"I presume they are looking for you also?"

Baelar nods.

"Even more risk then. But for the memory of my brother, and that is all mind you, in honour of him we will do it. Come with me. I will take you to the camp and you can meet the others."

"I have to return to the city." Jarel helps Zora with her headdress. "I will get word of when the execution will be."

Zora nods and then stepping forward throws her arms around his neck.

"Be safe."

"I will, child." A touch of her cheek and he is gone.

The rebel's camp is based in a selection of caves hidden deep in the hillside. There are twenty of them in all, mostly men, but there are a few women also. Although Zora is the youngest, they seem to follow her authority without question. They all look at Baelar with suspicion at first, but as Zora tells his tale their suspicion is replaced by sympathy. They all want to help free the man who dealt Officer Lichen the death card.

They talk long into the night, huddled around a fire drawing patterns in the dirt, discussing tactics and making plans. Baelar is weary but adrenalin is keeping him awake. It seems a very long time before Zora decrees that they all need rest. When he does lower himself onto the hard bed with the rough woollen blankets Baelar can hear the sounds of the village quietening around him, the occasional bark of a dog, the scratch of some rodent in the eaves, sounds that are strange to him, but that are as powerful as any lullaby as he drifts into a fretful sleep.

CHAPTER 23

The room falls silent. At the head of the table Aleric waits. Behind him Germin stands flanked by two soldiers; once they were his peers, now he is their prisoner.

Ratzka looks up.

"Death." His face is impassive. "Three days from now, at sunset, all will attend. In the square of the Grand Palace. All will see what happens to those who break our laws."

"How, Ratzka?" The member of the Council who speaks is a small man, thin with a narrow, mean mouth. "How will he die?"

"This is the question we have to answer." Ratzka pauses. "A swift end with electricity or an injection is out of the question. The crowd will want a spectacle."

"Bullets then." The excitement in the small councillor's voice makes Aleric feel sick to his stomach."

"Blade." Ratzka shakes his head. "Lichen died by the blade and so shall his murderer. Seven cuts he will receive, one for each life taken. Six where the blade penetrates the torso. The final cut will be to the throat."

"Why not take the head?"

Behind him Aleric can hear Germin breathing heavily. He feels anger starting to stir within him.

"With respect Council." His voice is calm, belying the agitation he feels. This man is a soldier; he deserves a soldier's death, not that of a common criminal."

"In some ways, I agree. Wise words as always." Ratzka nods in agreement. "But soldier or not, this man took the life of an Officer, and also that of a palace courtesan and several members of the same army he had pledged to serve."

"Who were all breaking our laws themselves. Who would have all faced the death sentence if they had been caught."

There was a pause, then Ratzka got to his feet.

"Yes, but the correct course of action was for this soldier to bring this issue to his senior officer, in this case you, General. Lichen would have been tried and justice dealt; his life was not for this man to take. Without order we do not have control. Without control what are we? Order upholds our laws and makes us what we are. We cannot lose that."

Aleric nods and bows his head, he knows that Ratzka speaks the truth, but to think of one of his men being used as a public example sickens him.

163

"But" Ratzka is still speaking, "General Aleric is right. Executing one of our own displays to our soldiers that breaking our law will not be tolerated; it shows to all who reside in the city that we make no exception. It will send a message to the rebels in the hills. But death is enough. The soldier will keep his head; but he will watch his life drain out of him after the final cut is made to the throat."

Aleric hears Germin whimper. Taking a deep breath, he turns and gestures to the soldiers flanking Germin to take him away.

"One more thing." Ratzka watches the departing figures. "He will be unmasked for execution. He is no longer a member of our army. Let his face, his fear and his pain be visible for all to see."

"Who will perform the task?" Aleric dreads the answer but feels he will know what it will be.

"You. General. You will be his executioner."

Germin cannot feel his legs as they take him back to his cell. His heart is beating so fast that he fears he cannot breathe. Wave after wave of anxiety wash over him. He knew he would die, but this? He had expected a firing squad, death by a needle, a clean end not the same sort of death usually saved for the rabble of the lower city: or for those who would oppose the might of the army hiding in the hills.

He feels, rather than hears Aleric behind him.

When the soldiers leave his confinement quarters Aleric remains.

"Not what I had hoped for." There is an edge of sorrow in Aleric's voice.

"No." Germin tried to speak but his voice disobeys him, and he croaks like an old man.

"As promised, I will make sure it is easy for you. I always keep my word."

Turning sharply on his heel, Aleric walks away.

Alone in his room Germin allows the tears to fall. This cannot be it. This cannot be the end. He thinks of Elle and her sing song voice, her kind eyes, and the trust she had placed in him. He thinks of Baelar and hopes he is safe in the barracks and not off on some foolhardy rescue mission.

There is one person he cannot think of. He cannot allow himself to think of Clara.

CHAPTER 24

"There will be no reason for you to attend."

Aleric's meal remains untouched on his plate. His wine glass is empty. Each glass that Elle has filled for him has been drained almost instantly.

"You can remain here and await your Mistresses' return."

Elle nods her thanks and backs away. As she does so, she bites her lip to suppress her anger. How can these men dictate who has the right to live or die? She is tired of taking orders. She longs to be free, to be back in the village. Now she sees that despite the comfort and safety this life gives her, even a meagre existence eked out of the dust is preferable to being a man's instrument.

Yes, she has Clara; she has clothes and plentiful food. She can bathe and sit in the gardens; she can walk outside the house along the streets. But what she does not have is the freedom to choose her future for herself.

Clara watches her friend as she leaves the room and feels her frustration. She has no wish to attend an execution and certainly not alone. She looks at Aleric who sits beside her with his face bare. His resolution to hide himself from Elle has failed, and Clara senses that for once he doesn't care. There is something heavier on his mind. His eyes are blank, staring into the distance. A distance she cannot see.

"Aleric." She reaches out and touched his hand. "Please. I have no wish to witness this thing. Let me stay here with Elle."

Aleric shakes his head.

"You will attend along with the women of the other generals and the members of the Council. It will be expected of you."

"Tell them I am sick. Anything?"

Aleric turns his eyes onto hers and for the first time since she has known him, she sees fear in them.

"Do you know how easily they would seek to have you replaced? Already they talk about the years we have spent together, how I have not found a new companion, I have not put you aside as is the accepted order of these things. If you do not attend it will be seen as an insult to our law and they will demand you gone."

"You wouldn't let them." She smiles and strokes his cheek. She can feel the clammy sweat beneath her fingers.

"Some things are beyond even my power."

Taking her hand in his he presses her lips to her fingers. "I do not want to do this, but I must. In the same way you must attend. For the sake of us, of this."

"What do you mean you don't want to do this." Clara stops short as realisation dawns. "You are the one who has to kill this man? A man who was trying to protect others?"

"Yes." There is a sorrow in Aleric's voice that she has not heard before. "It is something that I wish I could avoid; but the task falls to me, and it will not be pleasant. It is a brutal end."

"Then there is even more reason for me not to attend!" Clara jumps to her feet. "You wish me to watch you causing pain and suffering before eventual death? To watch you play the part of executioner?"

"No, I do not wish for it. It is what I have to do and in turn is what you have to do. Please Clara. Do not make this more difficult for me than it already is."

He pulls her into his lap and buries his face in her shoulder. She smells sweet and clean, and her scent calms his ravaged mind.

"I will need Elle." Her mouth is in his hair.

"No." Aleric looks up at her and she sees tears glinting in his eyes. "She cannot attend, I am sorry Clara, but you must bear this alone."

"Then." Clara reaches for the flagon of wine. "I

will be more in need of this than you."

Later, after Aleric is asleep, his head resting on her shoulder, Clara eases herself out of the bed and makes her way downstairs. In the small room where Elle sleeps a light still glows and she finds her friend awake.

"Elle," Clara sits on the edge of her bed. "Elle, please. I don't want to go to this execution, but I must. Please come with me. I can't do it alone."

"I have been told I can't," Elle continues to stare at the ceiling. "I have been given my orders."

"I can't do it alone," Clara repeats, as she lays down beside her and lays her arm across Elle's slender frame. It is the first time in many years they have lain like this.

Elle looks at her.

"You want me to disobey the mighty General?"

"Don't talk about him like that." Clara gives her a shove. "He is only following orders. He is a good man."

"A good man with the power to end our days with a nod of his head."

"Yes, but that is how this life is Elle. He chooses to keep us here, he allowed me to have you here with me, he could have refused it."

"Prisoners." Elle looks away. "Is all we are."

"What would you have us do?" Clara sits up. "Try and escape? Go out and hide in the Lower City and live our lives on the run?"

"Wouldn't that be better? To be free and take our own chances in life?"

Clara looks at her hands, at her painted nails and soft skin. On the cover beside her Elle's hands are rough and raw, nails chipped and dirty; reddened with the efforts of her labour. Their lives are very different. Somewhere inside there is a part of her that wants to be free, to be able to feel that the days of her life were not in another's control. But there is another part, a newer part, more recently formed, and much stronger: the part of her that cannot bear the thought of a life without Aleric.

Elle is watching her.

"You love him, don't you?"

Clara nods and tears prickle at her eyes.

"I'm sorry Elle. I know I shouldn't; I know he controls me and my life, but I do love him. I tried so hard not to, but it's too late."

"I saw." Elle confesses. "In the garden. For what it is worth Clara I believe he loves you also. That is a great risk for him, if anyone should see him displaying that level of emotion."

"I know." Clara takes her hand. "I don't like to believe that it's true but sometimes I really do see that he cares for me."

Elle breathes heavily and stares down at the covers.

"When we were girls we would dream,

remember? Of a man to love us and cherish us. But that was before; long before our lives changed. Now you have a man who provides and cares for you and my fate is linked to yours. No lover for me."

"Come with me." Clara looks at her pale face and huge eyes. "I am so scared Elle; I don't want to witness Aleric doing this."

"Then what do you suggest we do?"

"I will arrange it. I will have you collected by the maid of one of the governors. She will bring you to me. I will tell Aleric I was ill and called for you."

"Okay." Elle sighs. "I have to say that the thought of watching a soldier executed is not one that fills me with pleasure. Particularly not one who has tried to defend others."

"Thank you." Clara lays back down beside her and closes her eyes. They lie in silence, the room filled only with the sound of their breathing. Clara lets her mind wander back over all that they have been through since the day they were taken from the village. She sighs deeply.

"I am so glad you are here with me Elle, and that we have each other."

CHAPTER 25

Jarel drives with haste along the dusty track; time, he knows, is of the essence.

His day in the city has been spent listening to the gossip and trying to filter out the truth from the rumour. In the end it had been his own instructions that had given him the information he sought. Three days before Germin would die. Three days to plan a rescue that will change a man's fate. He has his doubts that they will succeed but for the sake of his son; in honour of his memory, they will try. As he approaches the village his mind is filled with memories; memories of a baby in his arms, of a child playing and laughing, of a body clad in rags at his feet. That had been the beginning of the end for his beloved Amora. The sight of her firstborn, a motionless corpse in the village square had broken her mind. It was after that day that the nightmares had started, the anger, the despair that drove her to insanity; the hours walking in her sleep and the countless searches to bring her back home to safety. Then one night the searches had failed. For hours they had climbed in the hills and walked on the dry plains. Nothing. Wherever his Amora was now, it was not in this life. Zora had taken it as she did all things, with anger. Then slowly the anger had become a resolve to change the way in which they were forced to live. It was this resolve, this determination that made her such a good leader. The men saw her passion and warmed to it.

He finds them huddled in one of the small stone houses and it is his daughter that he hears first.

"You cannot fire a gun?" The contempt in her voice makes Jarel wince.

"No." The voice that answers is quiet and ashamed.

"What did they train you in that place? How to fold the sheets on your bed?"

"I can use a blade. I can run for an hour without stopping. I can take a man's life with my bare hands. I had not yet been shown how to fire a gun."

"And you think you will get close enough to the metal-faced monsters to use your hands?"

Zora is laughing, her mockery fills the air of the small room and brings smiles to the faces of others.

"Then show him how to use a gun." Jarel walks through the door and slams it behind him. "Teach him and teach him fast. The man dies at sunset three days from now."

"Then I hope," Zora hands Baelar a gun, "you are a quick learner."

They work long into the night. Zora challenges Baelar again and again until, although his aim is still not good, he can fire the weapon without sending himself reeling backwards to the ground.

"You can defend yourself at least." Zora sits wearily. "Now eat, and rest."

"I can do neither," Baelar is staring at the night sky. In the darkness the world seems clean, renewing itself with the passage of time. "Both evade me."

"I understand." Zora stands behind him. "The brain never stops, does it? The memories, the fear? I know your pain."

Baelar looks at her. She has discarded her face covering in his presence now. Her face is proud and haughty. She has cheekbones that sit high and slanting on her face and a full wide mouth. Her hair is thick and knotted roughly at the back of her head. One errant curl has escaped and is lying across her long, slim, neck. Baelar has had no experience with girls. If he did, he supposed he would think her pretty; possibly something more than pretty. There was a strength borne of necessity that gave her a dignity many girls could not possess. In truth he would be more likely to call her beautiful.

"Come." Zora is aware of his gaze, "We must at least try and rest. Tomorrow, we plan how to get into the city."

Ten of them sit around a large, stained wooden table. The men, including Baelar have jugs of coarse ale. Zora has water. She claims she needs a clear head. On the table is a roughly made model of the city using stones and earth.

"Here." Jarel points. "This is where we will enter. There is to be a feast after the execution. They have called for three more trucks of provisions on the day. Three of us in each is all we can take."

"A feast?" Zora shakes her head. "So, who stays?"

"That is what we must decide." Jarel looks around the room.

"Him." Zora points at Baelar. "He is the least well trained."

"No!" Baelar is quick to his feet. "This is my mission. I want to be there."

"You will put us in even more danger!"

"I am a soldier." Baelar snaps, growing angry. "I can kill, and I know that city better than any of you."

"Zora." Jarel speaks softly. "You should remain behind."

He stares at her, his remaining child precious beyond words. He wishes to keep her safe, but he knows she will not stand down easily.

"No!" It is Zora's turn to raise her voice. "I am in command of this operation."

"Then we will draw lots and let fate decide."

Jarel also knows that words will not change her mind. "Chance will make our choice for us."

Zora watches as he gathers a handful of straws and breaks them into differing lengths and offers a stalk to each member of the group. A boy, barely old enough to lift the gun that he bears on his back draws the shortest straw. He nods quietly and leaves the room.

"It should have been you!" Zora hisses at Baelar.

"No." Jarel lays a calming hand on her shoulder. "This is Baelar's rescue; the condemned man knows him. He will come with him; with us he may resist."

"Very well." Zora shakes her head. "But if he puts us in danger, I will kill him myself."

So, the plan is set. Hidden in their cloaks they will each carry crude grenade canisters that will release smoke to confuse the crowds. One of the vehicles will need to be manned constantly so that they can get Germin and his rescuers to safety. Jarel volunteers, they need a driver who knows the routes out of the city, and someone who is not likely to be questioned leaving whilst the place is in chaos.

Once Germin has been taken to the place of his execution they will act; setting off the smoke canisters, firing shots into the air from every position; the aim is to cause panic and fear, to make the crowd move, to distract their attention from what is going on. The eyes of the soldiers will be on the disturbance and with a few more canisters fired to camouflage their view of the platform Zora and Baelar will have time to free Germin and get him to the vehicle. They will have cloaks and hoods to cover him as they attempt to get him through the crowd. There is one issue that remains: getting the extra person out of the city.

"If we can cause enough havoc," Jarel speaks slowly, "one may hide in the rear of the vehicle. We will have time. In fact, perhaps it is better we conceal Baelar's friend there. He is too easily recognised. They will not search the rear of the trucks; all their attention will be diverted."

"If it is not diverted," Zora is afraid but hides her fear behind angry eyes. "If we fail, I will be for the breeding houses and you for the executioner's blade. The crowd will have the pleasure of watching two men lose their lives and not one."

Jarel moves to a cupboard in the corner of the room and pulls out a small box. Inside it is a pile of black pills.

"No." he says grimly. "If we fail then we will all die together."

CHAPTER 26

The pale dawn covers the cell walls with a dim orange glow. Germin sits and watches the shadows fade away, knowing that when they reappear his time on this planet will be coming to an end.

He begins to shake, uncontrollable shivers that race each other across his skin; his mind is spinning as giddiness washes over him; he convulses and heaves but his retching retrieves nothing but an acid that burns his throat.

He has eaten nothing for days.

He is ashamed of his fear, ashamed of the dread that overwhelms him. He is a soldier, he has been trained to fight, to maim, to kill, but he has not been trained to die. To meet death in a battle is one thing, to stand and await the first blow that will be the beginning of his end is another. The sound of footsteps at the door makes him leap to his feet, backing into the wall, clinging to the last lingering shadow.

Aleric enters quietly and waits for the guard to leave before he speaks.

"I always keep my word."

He hands Germin a small syringe filled with a white liquid.

"When the sun starts to set use this. You will hear them starting to gather in the square, that will be the time. When they come for you, this will be taking effect. I promise you will feel and know nothing."

Germin sees his own hand shaking as he takes the syringe. He looks up with wide eyes and stares into the impassive gold metal face.

"Thank you." He mumbles.

"As I said, I always keep my word."

"Baelar?" Germin can feel the tears sliding down his cheeks, he cannot stop them.

"No sign." Aleric shrugs his shoulders. But we will find him, I promise, he can't stay hidden forever."

"Thank you."

Aleric turns to leave and then hesitates.

"Remember what I told you Germin, use that. You will feel nothing."

Germin nods, staring at the syringe in his hand.

Will he have the courage to use it? He doubts it. Not knowing that this will be his final action; that afterwards there will be nothing but oblivion. He looks at Aleric's powerful arms as he pulls the door shut and imagines the damage a blade will do in his strong hands. Imagines the pain as each thrust cuts his flesh. Somehow, he must find the courage.

The door clicks closed, and he hears Aleric's footsteps as he walks away.

"Look after her." He whispers.

Elle twists a final lock of hair into the pleat and fastens it with a gold clip. Onto it she attaches the sheer silk veil that will cover Clara's nose and mouth. Clara's eyes are lined with black; her lids glint golden; she wears a sheer silk dress of emerald green and over it she will wear a green and gold cloak, the neck trimmed with fur. She is staring at her friend in the mirror, her eyes wide.

"I don't want to do this Elle." She clutches at her dress as if it is choking her. "To see Aleric kill this poor man."

"I have no desire to witness it either."

"I know. But if we are together it will help. The maid of the counsellor will be alone, she is going to stop at the gate for you. When you get to the square follow her and you will find me."

"What if the General should see me?"

"He will not know Elle; you will arrive with the maid and leave with her. You will be here waiting long before we return from the feast."

"A feast," Elle scowls. "A feast to celebrate ending a man's life. How can you do it Clara? How?"

"I have to." Clara lowers her eyes. "If I don't, the

next execution I attend could well be my own."

Aleric waits for her at the door. She is as beautiful as the day he first saw her in her dirty clothes, hair wild, eyes proud and angry. As she passes him, he can smell her scent, sweet and flowery. On any other day he would be filled with desire. Today he is filled only with dread. They travel in silence. No touch on the arm, no finger laying gently on her thigh. Clara can see from the tension in his muscles that he is nervous.

"Have you done this before?" She whispers.

"No." Even his hollow voice is alien to her. "I have sent men to their death before this with an injection or a single bullet. But this, this is something else. You do not know how much I wish the task didn't fall to me."

"Then let us hope it is over swiftly. Make it quick. If they want a spectacle, don't let them have it on your account." Clara looks out of the window at the crowds that are filling the streets. "All these people! What pleasure can they get from watching a man die!"

Aleric follows her gaze. Their way forward is blocked by waves of people heading for the square; flanked on either side by the black faced soldiers of his army.

"They are not here by choice." He says grimly." They have been ordered to attend. This is a display of the law and what happens to those who break it."

He can see her eyes as she watches the crowds, and they widen in horror as the vehicle pulls into the square, and she sees the execution platform and the raised seating placed all around it. For the first time that day he takes her hand.

"It will be okay."

She looks at him.

"How, Aleric, will this ever be, okay?"

She watches him walk away from her and begins to climb the steps. The other women were already seated. Veiled, gowned, and scented. They watch her as she takes her seat. The row behind is clear awaiting the arrival of the maids. The woman beside her is one she has met before; she is the companion of a member of the council.

"If it makes you feel better," she whispers, "I have no wish to be here either."

Clara swallows and nods her thanks.

The woman is looking along the line of faces. So many are young, pretty, new replacements for women who had been exchanged. Women who no longer drew breath.

"Pretty young things, aren't they?" She nods to Clara. "Be careful, they will all have eyes on that General of yours."

Clara watches Aleric as he walks onto the platform. He is speaking to Ratzka and the other Governors. She looks around and frowns. Ratzka's woman is nowhere to be seen.

"Gone." Her companion follows her gaze. "She hasn't been seen for weeks."

Clara bows her head.

"Do you think one of these is her replacement?"

"Possibly, although he has been frequently absent from Council lately."

"You think he is ill?"

"That is the belief. He is pushing hard for someone to join the Council. Someone who can take his place. We all know who he favours."

Clara nods and watches the object of Ratzka's favour. As if drawn by her stare he turns and looks towards her. She lifts a finger and nods. The figure nods in return and turns to face the crowd.

"There are rumours." Her neighbour whispers, "rumours that the General has feelings that a man in his position should not have. Feelings for you."

"No." Clara shakes her head. "He fulfils his duty at the breeding houses. I am his companion, his accessory, nothing more."

"And his confidant?"

"Of course. Although he shares very little." She lied.

"Be careful. I would not want to see your face replaced with another."

The conversation between them ends and Clara watches, waves of sickness threatening to overwhelm her as the crowd continues to grow. A sickness growing not only from the dread of what is about to happen but from her own fear. Her eyes constantly return to Aleric. She must be careful. Perhaps they have been too free with their affections in public; touching, linking arms, holding hands. She must be careful.

There is movement behind her, and two women take their seats, one wears a large black hood that almost covers her eyes and a black face covering.

"I'm here." Elle whispers.

"Thank the gods." Clara reaches backwards and takes her hand. "Have you ever seen anything like this? It sickens me. Why were you so long?"

"The road was blocked, a provision truck had broken down, we had to pass through the lower city."

Ratzka is standing. The crowd, which until now had been creating a buzz of noise, falls silent.

The execution is about to begin.

The cell door swings open.

Four guards enter, masked and armed.

Germin stands to face them, unsteady on his feet, sweat beading his brow. He sways and falls against the wall.

At his feet, hidden underneath the bed is a small syringe.

It is empty.

CHAPTER 27

"Move it!" The soldier waves his gun at Jarel. "Come on. Hurry!"

"It won't move." Jarel shrugs his shoulders. "I am sorry, but I am going to have to wait here for help."

The soldier snarls and turns away, signalling for assistance. With a wave he dismisses the line of vehicles behind Jarel and one by one they turn creating a metal snail that moves slowly through the lower city. Jarel watches as the soldier pushes through the crowd, hand raised.

"Now!" He hisses. "Quick!"

Two figures jump from the side of the truck and quickly disappear into the gathering crowd. Jarel looks up. High on the roof of the Palace something glints in the sun. Across the square to his right another light flickers. Part of their group are already in position; the others have made their way deep into the masses of people that are flocking towards the square. He lifts the engine cover and begins to pull wires, muttering and cursing loudly, trying to convince the returning soldier of his efforts to affect a repair. Pocketing a small rubber pipe, he shouts above the noise.

"Is help coming?"

"Not yet." The soldier shakes his masked head. "Too many people. We will have to wait until this is over."

"As you will." Jarel nods. "I will keep trying, but I just drive the machine, I don't build it."

At least there is no danger of an army mechanic arriving soon. All around him the soldiers are becoming distracted. A black vehicle is pushing its way through the crowds towards the rear of the platform.

It is time.

Baelar crouches in the shadows at the side of the square; he keeps low, hood pulled hard forward over his face. He watches the black vehicle as it passes, so close that he can smell the heat of the engine. He knows what it carries. His stomach lurches and spinning round he heaves against the wall. Taking deep breaths, he steadies himself. His fingers close around the blade at his belt. On his back he can feel the weight of the gun, hidden beneath his cloak. He thinks of Zora positioned at the front of the crowd. He had watched her, lithe and slender, weaving her way through the mass of people away from him. His eyes scan the tops of the buildings that surround the square. Barely visible against one of the pillars close by he spots a shadowy figure, another of their group waiting, avoiding attention. Opposite him in the front of the square, backed by the facade of the Grand Palace, is the execution platform, beside this are rows of seats. Seats filled one either side with people in fine clothes. Behind them are more women, all women, no men, all plainly dressed and looking downwards; their eyes never raise to take in the scene in front of them. One woman in the front row catches his eye; clad in emerald green with a gold veil. Even from this distance Baelar can see her elegance and grace. Her wide eyes, just visible above the veil, are fixed on a lone figure standing on the platform.

General Aleric.

Baelar stares at the gold mask, dazzling in the sunlight and feels the beginning of hatred growing within him. How can Aleric, the man every boy in the barracks is taught to revere, be the one to end Germin's life? The words of Ratzka are booming across the packed crowd. Baelar doesn't listen. He is moving silently along the wall to his place. Beyond the platform, framed by one of the stone arches that surround the square, he can see Jarel's truck. Nerves tighten in his throat once more and fear threatens to overwhelm him.

He must be strong. He must push his fear down into the depths of his mind and focus; he has spent the last years of his life training to be a soldier; today he is becoming that soldier, not of the army that raised him but of justice. Justice for Germin, for Jarel's lost son, for all the other boys tormented by Lichen and for himself. If he has any chance of a life where he can be at peace, he needs to do this. Today, for the first time in his short life he has a job to do.

The door of the black vehicle swings open, and the crowds fall silent.

Two soldiers step out, each holding the arms of a stooping figure. The figure is staggering, it seems unable to walk. It is shrouded in a black cloak and hood, hidden from the view of the clamouring crowd who press forward as one. Baelar catches his breath, his heart is racing so fast it is making him feel faint. He looks down at his feet and tries to calm himself. As he looks back up, he sees the soldiers stop.

General Aleric nods and the black cloaked figure is turned to face the crowd. His arms are pulled behind his back and he is tethered tightly to a single metal post. Aleric pulls a blade from the belt at his waist and stands, rigid, hesitating, the steel in his hand catching the fading light as the shadows begin to move across the square.

A silence creeps through the crowd.

One soldier pulls off the cloak and reveals the man beneath.

There is a moment of stillness.

Then an inhuman scream splits the air.

The second the scream reaches his ears Aleric knows who has made it. He stares at the stooping figure of Germin, at the deep red hair and tousled curls; at the clear green eyes, hazy and drugged, but still the same as other eyes he has looked into; and he knows. The thought he has pushed to the back of his mind for so long is right there before him. He has asked himself this question so many times and he has convinced himself it was only his imagination. But this is no coincidence of geography. No two people could be more alike. He turns and looks towards the seating, seeking confirmation that he could somehow be mistaken, that this is not her brother standing before him waiting to die.

But Clara is gone.

CHAPTER 28

Chaos.

Confusion.

Smoke fills the air, stinging his eyes and blurring his vision but Baelar knows now is the time to act. He runs, bending low to the ground and jumps lightly onto the platform. Gunshots sound all around him, screams and cries echo off the Palace walls as the crowd tries to force itself through the arches and out of the square.

It had happened so swiftly in the end.

The second that Germin's face had been revealed a woman had screamed. The scream had hung in the air for a long time and drawn the attention of everyone. Except for Zora who had spotted the unexpected opportunity and launched a series of canisters into the crowd. Within seconds the square had been filled with smoke and the smell of fear. The crowds had panicked and started to flee; and now the soldiers were too intent on locating their attackers to spot a shadowy figure creep onto the platform.

Baelar hesitates. General Aleric is to his right.

But the general is not joining this fight against an invisible enemy, he is staring at the rows of seating. He stands immobile and Baelar can see that his blade has fallen from his grasp. For this one moment in time the great general is left unarmed. Staying low, almost crawling on all fours until he reaches the tall metal post Baelar finds that Germin's hands are chained in place. He curses under his breath; how is he to free him now? Crouched on his haunches he hacks at the chain with his blade, but it makes only a meagre scratch. Then there is another figure beside him; there are hands working swiftly, wielding a long, thin bladed knife that twists inside the lock until it snaps free.

"Hurry." Zora hisses. "We need to move fast; we cannot distract them for too much longer."

Germin leans heavy in their arms as they half drag him to the rear of the stage. Now the smoke-filled air is being fed by a fire which licks at the walls of the Palace.

"Fire?" Baelar glances at Zora.

"Not us." She whispers, "but be thankful for it."

Baelar nods; the attention of the army has now been distracted by the fire and they are aiding the governors and councillors from their seats, evacuating them to safety. On the opposite side of the square the women are having to free themselves.

Only one man is still yet to move. General

Aleric is motionless, staring at the emptying seats, oblivious to all around him.

Elle pulls at her friend's hand and starts to drag her down the steps.

"Clara. Clara, come on, we need to move!"

Clara is sobbing; unable to draw breath. The shock has made her vomit, and her luxurious green cloak is stained. As Elle guides her through the throng, she can feel her shaking. There is no time to calm her or show her compassion. The only thought in her mind is to get them both away from the square and whatever has caused this disruption. As she weaves a path towards an exit out of the square she glances backwards; on the platform, just visible through the smoke she sees three figures moving away from the spot where Germin had been chained. One is stooping and staggering and covered in a black cloak.

"This way. Quick"

Changing direction, she begins to fight her way towards the Lower City. Over the heads of the masses in front of her she can see the three figures have already reached the edge of the square and are pushing themselves into the crowds, using others as a shield. Soldiers are walking towards the platform; it will not be long before they realise their prisoner is taken. Something inside Elle is trying to surface. Something she keeps hidden but feels every day as it fights to get out. This is it.

This is her chance to rid herself of this enslaved existence she is being forced to live. She darts to one side and ducks into an alleyway pulling Clara behind her. There are people here also, but the progress is quicker. Staying close to the wall she halts at a junction. Peering cautiously out of the alleyway she can see a truck blocking the road. As she watches three shadowy figures emerge from the crowd and climb into it.

The truck grumbles and splutters then bursts into life. It is beginning to pull away and take with it her only chance of freedom. Grasping Clara's wrist, she begins to run dragging her friend behind her. The truck is turning. It has changed direction and is heading towards her.

She steps into the road; arms raised and stands in its path.

Jarel curses and slams hard on the brake.

Stupid Woman!

"Move!" He hangs out of the window. "Quickly."

"Take us!" The woman throws back her hood and looks at him with candid eyes. She is tall and thin with fair hair woven into a plait. He can see from her attire that she is a maid. The woman beside her is weeping, eyes downcast; her clothing speaks of status and power. As he runs his eyes over her, she wipes her face and looks up. Jarel starts.

"By the gods NO!" He begins to creep the truck

forward. "Do you wish me to set a date for my own execution? I know who she is. You want me to have the gold-faced general chasing after me?"

"I know what you have in the back of your truck," Elle is below the window, her voice low. "I know what you have done."

"So, what will you do, you crazy woman? Call for the soldiers and get us all killed?"

"Not if you help us." Elle's voice is calm, so calm that her next words chill him, but he senses she speaks the truth. "But I would rather die than return to the life I have been forced to lead. I cannot live with them anymore. If you do not take us, then this will still be my last day in this place. Also, you should know, that the man you hide in the back is her brother."

Jarel stares at the weeping woman. His compassion wants to help them, but his fear prevents him.

"I am sorry. He is safe, you are safe, let that be enough. Live your life out as her maid. There are worse options than that."

"Please," Elle is clinging to the door of the truck.

Jarel begins to creep forward.

"Drag me if you wish!" She cries. "Crush me with your tyres, I would rather that than serve these monsters anymore. Do you know what they do to women like me?"

Elle can sense the crowd behind her pressing

forward. The sounds of guns and the smell of smoke are everywhere; she can hear the voices of the soldiers now, trying to regain command. Jarel hears them also and knows that time is running short.

The door of the truck opens, and Zora climbs out.

"What is going on? Move quickly or we will all be dead."

"These women want to escape." Jarel nods towards Elle. "I am trying to leave but this one will not release her hold on the truck."

"Then drive over her! We need to go, now!"

"Tell her!" Elle looks at Jarel. "Tell her that the man inside is her brother. We cannot go back; there is nothing for us here. Tell her I will throw myself beneath your wheels rather than return to them."

Zora pauses. She hears the passion of Elle's voice, sees her worn red hands, her thin frame. She also sees the strength in her that can only be born of adversity. There is something about her, a quality that for one painful moment reminds Zora of the woman who had raised her.

"You we can take." She nods to the truck. "Her? Leave her to her fine clothes and her general."

Clara raises her head for the first time. Zora takes a breath. The pain in this woman's eyes is unlike anything she has ever seen; even in the eyes of her own mother when they brought her brother's body to the village. The pain that had been so strong it had driven her out of her mind. This was a woman whose world has been broken, whose every waking moment has been turned into lies. This is a woman who is in despair.

"Please." Even the voice is defeated, weak and timid. "Please just let me see him. Let me see he is safe? Let me tell him I will always love him, and I forgive him for everything."

Zora is looking over Clara's shoulder, her eyes fixed on a huge black machine making its way through the crowds.

"Get in," she snaps. "Quickly. Before it is too late for all of us."

Holding the door wide she helps Elle and Clara into the back of the truck and leaps light footed as a cat in behind them.

Inside the truck it is dark and cold. Elle shivers and tucks her cloak tight around herself. In the corner is a stooping figure, eyes staring down at his hands, motionless, not registering the presence of others around him. He does not move as his sister takes him in her arms. Beside him is a boy, not yet old enough to be a man, but his face carries a heaviness and care that far surpasses his years.

"Sit." He nods to Elle. "He will recover; he seems to have taken some kind of drug."

His words go unheeded, Elle is staring at Zora who has freed her hair from beneath her hood and removed her face covering.

"You are a girl!" She gasps.

"I am." Zora stares at her. "What of it? My name is Zora."

"Elle." Elle nods politely. "I apologise. It was just a surprise that is all."

Zora grunts in acceptance and sits down.

"This," she points to the boy beside her. "This is Baelar."

The truck moves slowly through the city pushing against the bodies that block its path. Jarel curses and squints through narrowed eyes as the sweat runs down his brow. His heart is pounding in his chest. Picking up these two women has caused an issue, they had hoped to leave the city with little delay, the chaos causing a distraction that allowed safe passage. This could mean problems; the army was using all its strength to regain control, soldiers were everywhere. All he could do was keep driving and hope.

Behind him five figures sit in the gloom of the rear of the truck in silence. Baelar's voice is the first to break it.

"Welcome." He says, "If we can help you to escape, we will."

The woman opposite him is staring, her pale eyes glittering with unshed tears.

"Baelar?" She croaks. "Baelar? Is that your name?"

"It is." He nods. "Why do you ask?

"It is an unusual name." The woman's voice is a whisper. "How old are you?"

"I am fourteen years."

The woman bites her lip, which is beginning to tremble.

"How did you come to be here?"

"My friend needed me." Baelar nods at the silent figure beside him. "Zora and her family came to my aid. I could not let him die."

"Friend?" The woman moves closer. There is something about her, her voice, which is stirring a sensation deep inside him. The shadow of a distant memory.

"Yes. He has always looked after me. I was a soldier once, like him. Or, at least, I was learning to be. Germin was always there, helping me, protecting me."

"I know." The woman's voice breaks and a sob bursts out of her. "Thirteen years ago, he promised to watch over you. I am proud of what you have done Baelar. So Proud."

"Promised who?" Baelar leaves Germin's side and moves closer to her. "What do you know?"

"Until the day he made that promise I knew everything. From that day on I would have known nothing; if not for him. Because he was watching you, I knew that you were alive and well. The day they took you my heart broke into two. I am your mother."

CHAPTER 29

Zora watches as the tale is told, albeit briefly. She can see in Elle's eyes that there is more pain; more anger, more hate that she is yet to share. She hears of the women being taken from the village, of their enslavement in the breeding houses, of Baelar's birth and subsequent removal from her. She never refers to Clara, Zora senses that her tale is for her alone to share when she feels it is right to do so. She watches as Elle's shaking hand reaches out for Baelar, the moment's hesitation and then her taking him into an embrace that goes on so long she thinks it will never end. The scene brings a lump to her throat as she thinks of her own mother, memories filled with love, of her brother before he was found lying bound and in rags in the village square. There is no bond, she thinks, greater than that of family. The masked monsters may have taken control of their lives but not of their hearts.

The woman called Clara has watched in silence, cradling her own brother in her arms, tears still sliding silently down her cheeks. She raises her hand to wipe them away and for the first time, Zora sees it: the mark, the tattoo on her wrist. A chill spreads through her and she lurches forward grabbing Clara's arm and staring as if trying to convince herself what she sees is not true. Green eyes look into hers and the silent message passes between them. They both know what the mark means.

Zora has no idea how far they are from the city border, but she knows this is a problem that cannot wait. Soon she will need to take her place in the front of the vehicle with Baelar to try and secure their safe passage out. Once they reach the outside of the city walls it will be too late. She throws herself at the front of the space they hide in as hard as she can, banging and shouting, hoping Jarel will hear her. She knows they will stop at some point, they must, it is part of the plan, but she needs to speak to him, and fast. Surely enough her efforts are rewarded, and she feels the vehicle begin to slow; releasing the inside door lock she peers out and seeing the streets still full of people leaps down and runs forward to the cab.

"Hey," Jarel spins around as the door swings open. "No hitchhikers!"

Zora sits down quickly and pulls her hood low over her face.

"We have a problem." She mutters.

"You think I don't know we have a problem?" Jarel shakes his head. "We are behind schedule;

people and soldiers surround us. We have a wanted man sentenced to death hidden in the back of the truck; if that wasn't enough, we now have two stowaways one of whom is the companion of General Aleric."

"Oh that." Zora shrugs dismissively. "That I can handle. This is worse."

"Worse!" Jarel stares at her. "What? How can anything be worse!"

"The women are tattooed."

"So?" For a second Jarel looks at her shaking his head; then as realisation sinks into his brain his eyes widen.

The vehicle comes to a sudden halt.

"Yes." Zora nods. "If they pass through the city gates without the chips being removed, they die."

"Then let them." Jarel wipes the sweat from his brow. "She claimed she would die rather than go back."

"It will not be pleasant."

"Then kill them now. That would be kinder. Give them the choice, die in the vehicle, or go back to their lives."

"If it were that simple." Zora stares out of the window and Jarel is surprised to see tears glistening in her eyes.

"What?"

"The one woman. Elle. She is Baelar's mother."

Jarel is staring at her.

"How? How is this possible? Does he know?"

"He did not. But he does now. The man he rescued had promised to watch over him. There's more to this tale, I'm sure of it but we don't have the time to find out."

"We put them out. The women." Jarel takes a deep breath. "Baelar can stay if he wishes. They will kill him if they find out what he has done. But we need to get out of this city alive."

"We need three in the front of this vehicle." Zora stares at the crowds still pushing slowly through the streets, guided by men in black masks. All are confused and anxious, wary of making one step out of line. "Three to match the paperwork we have. So, if we have one passenger hidden in the back why not three? The risk is the same."

"But the women will die. You know this!"

"I have an idea." Zora is sliding back out of the truck. "It will not be pleasant, but it is the only chance they have to live and be free."

Clara listens as Zora details her plan, listens but doesn't fully understand. Her mind is numb. Germin beside her is starting to rouse; when he had set eyes on her he had buried his head on her chest as he had done as a boy. Her heart had lurched, and compassion had overwhelmed her as she rocked him like a babe. As the initial hysteria and fear has subsided, she is being reminded of another whose head has lain on her chest, another whose arms have wrapped around her.

Aleric.

Germin, if he leaves the city, will be safe, she knows this; yes, they will search for him, wanting to seek vengeance, but in time they will turn their attention elsewhere. But what of her? What would her life be without Aleric beside her? What meaning would her days have, what would she do on the long dark nights without him to cling to for warmth and comfort? Without his strength to guide her through the days. But if she returns what will come of it? He will have looked for her, she is sure, he will have seen that she has fled. Her only chance would be to return to the house, now, to claim that she and Elle had got caught up in the panic at the square. But she would be alone. She knows without asking the question that Elle will not go back. Whichever choice she makes she will lose one of them.

Be it Elle or Aleric her life will change forever. Loosening her hold on Germin she places her head in her hands, her thoughts racing around her exhausted brain.

"Clara, Clara!" Elle's voice pierces through the fog of her mind.

"What." With effort Clara straightens and looks at her.

"Will you do it?" Elle is pointing to the tattoo on her wrist.

"Do what?" Clara narrows her eyes,

"You haven't listened, have you? I knew it. The brands, the tattoos. The chips inside them, if we try to leave the city with them inside us, we will die. We cannot leave the city. Our only option is to cut them out."

There it was. Embedded in her own skin lay the answer to her questions. The reason she needed to flee this truck and find her way back to Aleric.

"Cut them out?"

"Yes." Zora is wiping her long, narrow, blade with a cloth. "The chip is at the centre of the tattoo, it will be deep, it will be painful but if we bind the wounds tightly, we will make it to the medic in the village."

Clara hesitates.

"Cut them out." She repeats, her voice little more than a whisper. Looking down at her arm she runs her finger over the mark. It has been there so long she stopped registering its presence years ago.

There, embedded in her flesh is her reason to stay.

There, embedded in her flesh is the way she will die.

There will be no graceful old age for her, no years spent watching grandchildren play in the dirt, no gradual, steady demise to the grave. She already carries her death within her; be it now or in the future, her ending is always there. She hesitates. What will she have if she returns to Aleric? One year? Two? Ten? The words of the councillor's companion come back to her. A calm descends over her agitated mind and the fog that has encased her since the moment she had seen who was about to die lifts. She looks up, her eyes filled with clarity.

"Yes." She says quietly. "Cut it out."

CHAPTER 30

Baelar watches in horror as Zora pushes the blade deep into Elle's flesh. She holds her hand steady, pressed against the side of the truck, Elle's other hand is clinging tightly onto his own. Zora has torn a piece of cloth for Elle to bite on. For a second Elle is still, transfixed by the blood beginning to trickle from the wound, then as Zora digs deeper, she begins to shudder as her body reacts. Her jaws clench on the rag in her mouth and she squints her eyes tight shut. Her nails dig into Baelar's flesh, and he winces.

"Hold on," Zora is moving the blade in a square, like a butcher carving a joint of meat. "Not much longer."

"How do you know when you have it?" Baelar whispers.

Zora looks at him.

"When I reach bone."

Elle's mind is beginning to drift, hazy images dancing before her eyes: a baby in her arms, a tiny house in the hills, her parents smiling at her as she plays in the flowers, a darkness spreading over the land and a great cloud of dust, men in black metal masks and women being herded like animals into vast black vehicles. A faceless soldier is ravaging her body, then pain, unbearable pain as she fights to push another being out of her body. She fears the pain, it is too great, and she has no wish to fight it anymore. She begins to fade, waves of blackness washing across her mind.

"Elle." A voice she knows, but where is it coming from? "Elle. Come back to me?"

She opens her eyes and looks into a face that is so like her own. Kindness and warmth radiate from it. Baelar. The son she thought she had lost forever. He reaches up and removes the rag from her mouth.

"I am here." She smiles weakly.

"It is done." Zora lowers her blade.

Elle cannot look at the hole in her flesh as Zora wraps it, or at the blood staining her clothes, she can only look into the eyes of her child.

"At last," she murmurs. "At last, I am free."

Clara has watched the process with a sickness in her stomach. She knows it is her turn. She knows that by doing this she will have the chance of a free life, of an old age, but she also knows that it will remove her forever from Aleric. This is the moment when she will choose her own fate. An irreversible choice. But a choice that she herself is free to make, not one imposed on her by others. Looking into Zora's eyes she nods and moves from Germin's side. He murmurs, still deep in his drugged state and reaches for her. She hesitates.

"It's okay." Baelar releases his mother's hand and takes Clara's. His touch is soft and gentle, comforting. "I am here."

Clara's skin is pale and very delicate. The instant the blade penetrates her skin the blood flows fast. Zora curses as she cuts frantically, unable to see her way through the blood, trying to act swiftly before too much is lost. Clara's tattoo mark is bigger than Elle's; she will need to cut away more flesh.

"I am sorry." She mumbles as a high-pitched whine escapes Clara's cloth gagged mouth.

Clara watches her through hazy eyes as she mops frantically at the gaping wound to give her sight.

Blood on the floor.

Pools of deep red blood.

Clara has lain in her own blood before this. She breathes deeply and the image of a face hovers before her eyes. A face with golden hair, greying at the temples and ice blue eyes.

"My love." She mutters, but the vision is fading, moving slowly away from her until he is far from her sight.

He is gone. Aleric is gone. No more will she lie in

his arms and smell the heat of his skin; never again will she feel the power of his body next to hers; she sobs. There is a soft thud, and a square of flesh falls to the floor. There is something being wound tight around her arm. Zora sits up and moves away from her. Her face is pale, her hands dark with blood.

"It is done."

The two women, blood drained and tired, sleep with arms bound tight, red patches seeping silently through the wrappings. Beside them the red-haired soldier also sleeps the drug slowly leaving his system. Zora turns to Baelar.

"Cover them with sacks. All we can hope is that they do not take too much notice of this vehicle when we try to leave."

They feel the truck beginning to slow as it prepares to halt. Zora unlocks the door and opens it just enough to peer through. In her hand is a blood drenched sack; as she steps out of the door, she flicks it beneath the wheels. Jarel looks at them as they climb in. Zora's hands are black with drying blood.

"Hoods up." He commands. "Face masks on and keep quiet; and by the gods keep your hands out of sight."

The soldiers watch the vehicle approaching, guns raised. Jarel's heart is pounding so hard he fears they will see its movement in his chest. He swallows and tastes bile. Nodding, he slows beside the first soldier and lowers the window.

"Identity." The command is brisk.

Jarel hands over three cards hoping that the shaking of his hand will not betray his fear.

"Where were you some half an hour ago?" The soldier's metal face is black, so black that not even a glint of eyes can be seen.

"Ah," Jarel shrugs. "I was stuck in the crowds; stupid thing would not start. I was the problem blocking the entrance to the square. Some of your colleagues kindly came to help but it had corrected itself."

"So, you saw what happened in the square?"

"No. I had my head in this engine. I heard a lot of shots and then there was smoke; these two were afraid so as soon as this thing fired up, we pushed on through the lower city to avoid the crowds. We had been delivering food for the banquet, the youngsters here were scared, thought the rebels would see us as a target."

"How do you know they were rebels?"

"Who else would it be? Not one of your kind I wager. A dissatisfied servant with a gun? No, rebels they were."

Without warning Baelar doubles over in his seat and retches. Vomit pours out of him covering his clothes, his shoes and the footwell of the vehicle.

"Nerves." Jarel shrugs at the soldier. "He has been this way since he was a child."

Jarel sees the soldier shudder with distaste.

"You want to check in the back?" With one hand Jarel pats Baelar's back as he vomits again.

"By the gods no." The soldier steps backwards. "Off with you. He stinks. Make sure you clean that vehicle before you use it again."

"Oh, I will." Jarel smiles and drives slowly forward.

As they pass through the gates, he sees that the drones which normally circle the perimeter scanning the vehicles with heat sensors are gone, searching no doubt for the cargo he has in the back, but thankfully looking in the wrong place. As he begins the slow climb out of the city Jarel opens the window wide and chuckles.

The soldier is right. The truck stinks.

CHAPTER 31

Aleric stands in the doorway and listens. Silence. A silence that presses on him, seeping into his every pore. The house is as he left it this morning.

Empty.

It has been six hours since the rebels had attacked the square and caused the disappearance of Germin. Six hours since he had looked to the seating and saw her place empty. Six hours of searching for the rebels, six hours of intimidation and demands. The searches had revealed nothing. Deep down Aleric is now convinced of two things. One is that the man he had been told to execute was Clara's brother. Two, that the boy Baelar was behind the attack. How he had found the rebels that have helped him Aleric cannot understand, what he can understand is that Lichen had damaged enough of his pupils over the years to have no shortage of enemies looking for revenge. Willing to risk their own battered lives to save a man that they saw as a hero. He has trawled the city for Germin but has found no trace of him.

Even a few brutal executions have not loosened the tongues of the inhabitants of the lower city. He believes that Germin is no longer in the city. How they have got him out of the city walls would eventually come to light, but for now he has to admit that his quarry is gone.

All the time that he had been searching he had been comfortable in the belief that Clara would be safe at home waiting for him. The initial shock of her disappearance had been rationalised by his methodical brain. Of course, she would flee the square and seek safety. Elle would be with her, the other women. She was his woman; any soldier would assist her in safe passage home. Even if she had taken refuge inside the walls of the Palace, by now she would be at home waiting for his return.

But she is not.

The house is still and empty and he knows without question that no one has set foot through its doors since he left that morning. He goes to call her name but knows it is pointless; instead, he walks from room to room, hoping against the remains of his fading hope that he will find her sleeping in a chair or laid in their bed; bathing away the trauma of the day in a deep soothing bath. But there is nothing. Only the silence which deepens until it is digging at his brain and tormenting him.

Going downstairs he lays his gold mask on the table and reaches for a flagon of wine. In the cover of darkness, broken only by the dim light of the stars he walks into the garden and waits.

The pale light of dawn wakes him, a feeling of warmth on his skin. As he opens his eyes he keeps very still and listens.

Nothing.

A weight unlike anything Aleric has experienced lays on his chest. A great yawning chasm of emptiness is growing inside him until he feels that it will overcome him. He fears he will not be able to bear it. He has no need to ask himself where she might be. He knows where she has gone.

A thought rushes into his mind, a thought that stabs at him and he doubles forward placing his hands over his eyes. Warm tears seep through his fingers, and he tastes salt as they stream down his cheeks and reach his lips.

She is gone. Not just from him but forever.

If she has tried to leave the city, then she is dead.

Aleric throws his head back and howls like a wounded animal. Leaping to his feet he begins to throw anything within his reach. Only when tables are broken, glasses are smashed, and doors ripped from their frames does he stop. He looks at the damage around him with emotionless eyes. Let it rot. Let the windows break and the garden fade. It was all for her and she is gone.

With a trembling hand Aleric lifts his gold mask from the floor and clicks it back onto his head. He takes a deep breath and draws himself up. Here he can hide, here behind the mask he can wait for the pain to pass, he can shed tears of grief that no one can see; the great General void of all visible emotion will hide his heartbreak from the world. He does not look back as he walks through the door and leaves the place that has given him so much happiness.

As he gets into his vehicle something catches his eye. A comb, green and gold lying on the floor. He picks it up and stares at it, seeing in his mind's eye it sitting in her copper curls. Slowly he tucks it deep into his leather uniform. His heart twists as he thinks of her. He will send his men to search the perimeter of the city. There must be a body. He will have her brought to him.

Then he can at least look on her dead face and say goodbye.

CHAPTER 32

Clara wakes slowly and hears the dull whispering of voices. She feels weak and her mouth is dry. Her right wrist is heavily bound and is being pierced by constant stabs of pain. For a few moments she has no knowledge of where she is. Then they return, the incoming flood of memories that swell and swell until they threaten to drown her. The bed she lies in is hard, the sheets coarse. It feels alien and empty. It is the emptiness that drowns her most swiftly. The knowledge that her bed will now always be empty.

She sits up, a little lightheaded, and looks around her. A small bare room, one wooden chair, a table, a jug containing some water, drawers with handles long rusted and hanging loose. So different from her room at home. The home that is no longer hers.

Clara begins to cry. A high-pitched keening that causes the spines of those who hear it to run with chills, for their hairs to stand upright on their skin. One who hears it acts. They run to her room and enter uninvited. A pair of arms enclose Clara, and hands begin to stroke her hair gently. She opens her eyes and looks up into a mirror. A mirror that lives and breathes. This is why she is here. This is why she is filled with an all-encompassing pain.

"It is okay sister." Germin says softly. "I'm here Clara, it is behind us now, all of it."

It is a week before Clara feels well enough to leave the room; be it weakness or misery she cannot tell but her energy has left her. Elle comes to see her often. Her eyes grow brighter each day and slowly the pallor that has adorned her cheeks is being replaced by a glow. A glow that had left her some fourteen years ago. It is she that encourages Clara to move.

"Look at you." She scorns. "Wallowing in your own filth, you reek Clara. Get up, wash, change your clothes. We are free Clara, free to live as we please!"

Clara nods and looks away.

"Okay." Elle turns from her and leaves the room. "Lie here and rot. I cannot understand how you would prefer life with a man who would kill you with a nod of his head to waking each morning free to live as you choose."

In the empty room the words repeat over and over in Clara's head. Yes, she is free, but freedom will not replace what she has lost. It is not the fine trappings and finery she grieves for; it is the comfort of another human being holding her in their arms at night, the sensation of their lips on hers. She knows that for her, in this lifetime there is only one who could take that place. But he is far from her now, and with him the power that he held over her. Her life is now for her to control.

Her life. A life that is all she has.

It is some hours later that Clara enters the room where they all sit. Elle's words have stirred her. Her friend is right, she has lain and wallowed in misery long enough, she has to try and move forward as to go back is impossible. She has washed and covered herself with the harsh brown cloth that serves as a material for the dress she wears. Her hair is wound into a knot at the back of her neck. She is unrecognisable as the woman who has sat in her finery beside the general for so many years. Elle is wearing trousers made of dark green fabric, she sits like a man straddling a chair talking to Baelar who sits close. Clara feels a pang of envy. She will never look into the eyes of a child and know it belongs to her.

Zora sits near them, watching them with animated eyes. Clara sees her hand straying occasionally towards Baelar's thigh and recognises the very beginnings of youthful lust. Everyone is happy. Everyone is free. Why then can she not shift the cloak of heaviness that sits on her heart? Germin watches from the shadows, partly hidden in the corner of the room. His eyes glint softly in the half light. She catches sight of him and as she does so the unwanted memories come flooding back, overwhelming her. She spins on her heel and runs through the door.

A dusty deserted street greets her, a row of ramshackle houses with broken doors and shuttered windows. In the corner of the courtyard in which this house stands is a dirty brown dog. Thin, with mottled fur and patches of bare scaly skin it watches her approach with wide eyes and cowers. Clara crouches low and reaches out her hand. Waves of compassion wash over her, here is another creature lost, confused and out of place in this world. Slowly the dog creeps forward, back hunched, slinking low to the ground. Its nose reaches for her hand and sniffs the bloodstained bandage on her wrist. It creeps closer, head bowed and allows her to touch its skinny frame. As she gently strokes the matted head its tail begins to move from side to side.

Here, in the midst of her despair, she has found a friend.

CHAPTER 33

For two more days they linger in this derelict place. Clara spends her time sitting in the courtyard with the dirty brown dog. She names him Caval, for the dog that had been hers as a child and as each hour passes so his trust in her grows. As his trust grows so does her belief in being alive. He is her focus, her purpose behind opening her eyes in the morning.

Germin watches them and knows that she is not ready to be as they once were. Her initial horror of seeing him on the verge of death has passed and the memory of what happened lies like a giant chasm between them. He hopes it will pass and that she will in time understand, if not forgive, his actions and see that he too had been a prisoner. The morning that they are due to leave, he finds her sitting in the dirt with the mangy cur she has befriended.

"Clara." He stands back, hesitant. "We should talk."

"Why?" She looks at him through the tangle of her hair which is fast losing its shine. "What is done is done."

"When you were," Germin begins, determined to speak the words that he had turned over in his brain for so long. "When I came around in the truck you were holding me."

"Yes." She nods, "I had thought I was going to watch you die. I was terrified. I wanted to hold you and keep you here with me."

"But now you stay away from me, avoid me, we don't speak, you don't even look at me. Clara I am sorry. What happened in the breeding houses was not deliberate, it was an error, a giant mistake that I have tortured myself with ever since, but I didn't know who you were then! Do you not think that it has haunted me also? Can you imagine the horror I felt when I realised who you were?"

"The horror you felt?" She stares at him. "You can have no idea, not even begin to have an idea of what I went through! I have told myself so many times that this was not your doing Germin, how could you have remembered me after all those years? You were a child. But it was the violence of it all that made it worse. The knowledge that my brother thought of women as nothing more than objects for his gratification. Is that how you treated all the women?"

Germin's cheeks colour and he sits on the ground beside her. Caval curls his lip, showing his teeth and a faint growl comes from his throat.

"I did what we were taught. I knew nothing else.

You must know that after all the years you spent with the general."

"He is different." She says shortly.

"Is he?" Germin shakes his head. "Different. The mighty gold faced General Aleric who was going to execute me for ridding the world of a monster."

"It was his job; he was carrying out orders. Living by the laws of that godless place."

"As was I!" Germin rubs at his face, irritated. "Do you think I was acting differently to any of the other boys who had been brought up by those freaks?"

Clara stares at him and sees the anguish in his eyes. She reaches over and touches his leg lightly.

"Maybe not. But when I saw your scar, realised it was you, it devastated me Germin. It haunted me. It makes me sick to the stomach when I think of it."

"As it does me." Germin takes her hand.

"No Germin. You will never feel as I did. You did not have to rid yourself of an unwanted child. The only child I could ever bear. The child of a man you knew to be your brother."

Germin stares at her, his face slowly losing colour, his eyes widening.

"A child?" He whispers.

"Yes, Germin, a child. Our child. What kind of abomination is that? So many times, I have wondered what would have happened if I had not taken the drugs to rid myself of it. Possibly I would not have lived the life that I have had with Aleric, but I would have had something that I will now never know. A child in my arms. Something to love and caress, to feel that bond with however short. I am only half a woman. The part of me that nature intended I use to create new life was taken from me."

"By him." Germin snarls. "Yet still you defend his actions."

"But then I think," Clara is not listening. "What would it have been like if I had birthed the child? Would I have loved it or hated it, a constant reminder to me of what happened? Would I have spurned it and endangered my own life as a result? How could I have wanted it; with the replica of your face looking at me as I nursed it? So, then I believe that what I did was right, and my life has been how it was meant to be."

"Clara." Germin reaches for her hand.

"No." She pulls it away, reaching instead for the rough, matted fur of the dog beside her. "I know that what you did was your duty as a soldier. Nothing more, perhaps, as you say, that is how all men treat the women in that place. My experience has luckily been limited to Aleric and to you."

She looks at him.

"You are my little brother Germin. We have both been dealt a harsh fate and now perhaps it is the time to start again; to rebuild our lives. I love you as anyone would love their brother. I could not have watched you die. But it does not mean that I am ready to be as we once were. Not yet. I need time. There are wounds other than the one on my wrist. They all have to heal."

Elle finds them some moments later still sitting in the dust, Caval scrounging at their feet. Their faces are hollow and drawn with emotion and she knows what has been said. She spins on her heel and goes to find Baelar.

They need to go home. All of them.

The house is still as they left it. Nothing has changed, only the arrival of the layer of dust and grime that has settled over everything. The door creaks stiffly on its hinges as they open it, and a rush of tomblike air comes to greet them. On the wall the photograph of them still hangs, the waves still rolling behind them frozen in time in a faded image. Clara sits on one of the dirty chairs and stares at the floor.

How different could their lives have been if she had fought that day, the day they had taken Germin? Would they have been saved from the misery of the past years?

Germin is standing beside her.

"We all would have died." He reads her thoughts.

"Perhaps." She nods. "It may have been better for us all."

She looks up and sees Elle in the doorway, Baelar

stands beside her. How things have changed. Elle is now the one with love in her life. Maybe this is how it should be, she has taken her share of contentment and now it is the time for others to feel it. Her happiness, her love, all her emotions have left her. She has chosen freedom, the freedom to live and grow old and die as nature intends. A longer life, but an empty one, void of touch and passion.

Caval pushes his way through Elle's legs and walks cautiously into the room. He creeps softly to Clara and lays his head on her knee. For the first time in many days a smile touches Clara's lips.

She is wrong. Her life will not be an empty chasm. Love and affection lie at her feet.

CHAPTER 34

Aleric stares at the small hessian sack that the soldier has dropped onto the ground. The bag is black with dried blood and flies swarm to it. Inside are two pieces of flesh, beginning to decay. The stench hits his nose, and he heaves. The soldier is shifting nervously on his feet, fighting his own desire to gag.

"Have you scanned them?" Aleric's voice is abrupt and taut with emotion.

"Yes." The soldier nods. "One is definitely her."

He watches as Aleric stands, motionless, and looks at the sack.

Aleric feels the tide of despair gathering inside him. It is growing steadily, turning his skin hot and his heart heavy. Despite his horror at the thought of looking at Clara as she lay dead in front of him, the action would have closed the door on his emotions. Ended his pain. He could have grieved for her silently and continued with his work knowing that she was no more. That it was over. Forever. But this, he does not know how to deal with this.

She is alive. She breathes, she lives, she exists. But no longer with him. She has chosen to mutilate herself and leave the city rather than return to their life together. He has no idea how to feel, how to act. The thought of a life without her is challenging enough, but to know that somewhere outside the city walls she continues in a life that doesn't include him? How is he supposed to get through each day? Carry out his duties? He had believed that Clara shared his feelings, that theirs was more than an act for the world. Had he been wrong? No, he was convinced that her actions towards him had been genuine; and that made this rejection even harder to bear.

He knows there is only one thing that he can do. If he is to be able to continue living this life, then he must find her. He must make her face him and tell him how she feels.

Only then will he have peace.

Inside the Council chambers the air is warm and smells of stale bodies, of unwashed flesh. The ageing of the Council members comes with a price.

Ratzka's pale eyes, eyes that betray the man's growing weakness, are staring at him.

"So, let me understand this general. You want to leave the city and search for a woman?"

"Not me." Aleric hopes his voice will not betray his desperation. "Some of my men."

"Why?"

"They need to be brought to justice. The two women who helped the prisoner escape. Remember they will be hiding with the rebels. We need to stop this rebellion and this way, if you find one then you will find the other."

"But this woman was yours for many years was she not?"

"She was."

"Is there another reason you want her brought back here Aleric? I have heard the rumours; do you not have feelings of, how shall we put it, affection for her?"

There it is. Aleric knows he must be careful.

"No. I have no feelings for this woman. I want to demonstrate to those that would defy us, anywhere within this city, that they will be punished, whoever they are."

Ratzka nods.

"On that General I agree. But I tell you that if the prisoner had not been taken from us, I would not sanction this, the women could rot. What are they to us? One cannot bear children and would be ended when her time was done, the other is a serving girl, a maid, of no value. But this prisoner and those who freed him should be found. When they are, they will be taken to the square, and they will die. All of them."

"Of course." Aleric's head bows slightly.

"But there is one thing on which I must insist."

"What Governor?"

"The deaths must all be at your hand, including the death of your woman. You must be the one to take her life."

Aleric's heart thumps so hard in his chest that he fears the occupants of the room will hear it. He must agree. It is his only way of trying to find her. How he will deal with the aftermath he cannot think of now, but there will be a way, there will be some means by which he can have her back with him. But that is a challenge for another day.

For now, all he needs is to find her.

They search for five days, ten men working in rotation. They return every evening with the same result. They can find no trace of Clara, Elle, Germin or the boy Baelar. By now Aleric suspects that the merchant Jarel has an involvement in it; he has not been seen since leaving the city on the day of the execution; another man has brought the provisions to the Palace. Jarel had been one of the very few who were allowed to exit the walls in that afternoon of smoke and chaos. None of the governors know where Jarel's home is, only that he has delivered provisions to the city for many years. It could be close, or it could be days away. Frustration tugs at Aleric, his inability to locate Clara plays constantly on his mind. He believes he will have a better chance of finding her if he undertakes the search himself, but it would cause too many questions if he asked permission. Since the day of her disappearance, he has slept in the barracks; why would he want to sleep in a house that reminded him only of her? He cares little if he never walked through the door of that place again. As the days pass the man that Aleric has become begins to fade and threatens to leave only the soldier in its place.

Routine and discipline are the answer to all his problems, and he throws himself into his work. Emotion is shut from his mind. His men watch him and feel their nerves heighten in his presence. When the general had shared his home with the flame haired woman his nature had mellowed. He had been firm but fair. The Aleric who stands in front of them now is demanding, angry and lost.

The weeks roll by and normality, the life he had lived before Clara returns. In his head, Aleric has her dead and gone, a memory only, but his heart will not let go, rousing him in the middle of the night with dreams that make him want to scream and cry. It is late one afternoon when Ratzka summons him and as Aleric enters the hall of the Great Palace, he knows what route the conversation will take.

"Well, General." Ratzka has become thin and bowed, he stoops low when he stands, his ageing now rapid. "The time has come. I must step aside, and yet younger blood take my place on the

Council. Do I need to speak the words?"

"No." Aleric nods. "You do not."

"So, what is your decision? Has enough time passed? Will you remove your uniform and don the robes of a governor?"

Aleric hesitates, head lowered. So finally, it has come to this, the end of everything he has known. There will be no going back to the life he lives now, just as there is no returning to the life he had lived with Clara. But if he rejects the offer what will his future be? A continuation of his existence as it stands until old age prevents him from fulfilling his duties. As a governor he can influence the way in which the city is run and protect his men and the boys who train to replace them.

"It is a pity," Ratzka is speaking "That the move to crush the rebels didn't happen, events as you know took over. Maybe now is the time to try again. When a new general is elected, he can lead the search."

Aleric looks up.

"I promised to rid the hills of the rebel's Governor, and I shall. It would not be fitting for me to don the robes of the Council while the threat is still present."

"You can order it done Aleric, from the safety of inside the city walls. Let others take the risks you have carried for so long."

"No. The risk is mine to take. Because of my

slow actions we lost a prisoner, our position is weakened, our control will be questioned. I will complete this mission as a soldier not a governor."

"A month." Ratzka is ignoring him, "a month and you will be entered into the Council. That will give time to nominate your successor. In that time Aleric you can make your attempts to find these rebels, go and search yourself if you must. But also, in that month Aleric you must find a woman, the people need to see you with a companion."

Aleric breathes deeply. To refuse will cause issues but he has no wish to seek out or accept another woman.

"I will see if one can be found Governor. Thank you for the privilege you offer me."

As he walks away Aleric's mind starts to race. A month. He needs to act quickly.

CHAPTER 35

"Nothing." The soldier facing Aleric shakes his head and shrugs. "No signs of life. This village is deserted."

"Then we move on, further into the hills." Aleric is sitting in his vehicle, engine running.

"Yes sir."

"Gather the men." Aleric closes the window. "We go south."

From her position high in the mountain, hidden from their view by a range of low-lying bushes Zora watches them; she sees the slow-moving line of black vehicles and the direction in which they now head. She must warn her father, she needs to get back to the village and make everyone ready to leave. The men in masks are too close for comfort.

Aleric sees the tyre tracks in the ground as the line of vehicles reaches the top of the mountain. They have to be close by, the tracks have been made not that long ago. They first come across a ramshackle collection of crumbling houses with broken shutters. There are signs of life, ashes in the fireplaces, footmarks in the earth but every house is empty. He can tell that his quarry has been here, but it has already fled. The ashes lie cold, and the cupboards are empty.

"On." He tells his men. "They are deeper into these hills."

Miles ahead Zora and Jarel turn Jarel's truck downhill, away from the village where Clara and Elle hide. They must draw the soldiers away. As they drive Jarel is careful to leave as many tracks as possible, for the first time taking no caution. He drives quickly to protect their own safety whilst creating a diversion. At the bottom of the hill is a riverbed, he swings the truck onto it and bounces over the slimy rocks. The soldiers will follow him to the riverbed and quickly lose his trail. He will climb back up into the mountains when he knows it is safe.

An hour later Aleric sees the tracks leading downward and is about to follow them when something catches his eye on the opposite hillside. High up against the skyline is a gap in the rocks, an opening just big enough for a vehicle to pass through. In the gap something is moving, something small. He lifts his field glasses and sees the shape of a dog. He narrows his eyes at the creature, then he sees that something is moving behind it, a figure, albeit barely visible in the shadows. A sensation rushes over him, a feeling of recognition, of belonging and he catches his breath.

Behind him the soldiers all sit in their vehicles waiting for his command. For a moment he hesitates and looks back up at the rocks. Nothing moves. Had it been his imagination? Is it just his desire causing him to see things that were only the product of his tortured mind?

He looks down at the tyre tracks, turns to the men and points them downhill.

"They have gone this way. Follow them."

It is dark when the convoy returns to the city, and they have found no sign of the rebels. As the men make their way to the barracks Aleric hangs back. He cannot rid himself of the feeling that has haunted him since that moment in the hills. The figure still dances, small and distant before his eyes. Then his memory stirs, and he remembers a time when he had looked at that same gap in the rocks before; once many, many, years ago when he was a younger man and had not experienced the joys and sorrows of love. His heart begins to beat faster and adrenalin courses through his veins.

Tomorrow his time will be up, he will face the council and accept that his search has found nothing, that the rebels are long gone, and he will then remove his uniform for the last time and don the robes of a governor. Once that move has been made his days of freedom to leave the city will be over. As will his days of pining for Clara; he will be expected to take a new woman, a stranger will lie in his arms, will await his return each evening and offer their body for his pleasure, but there will be no love. If he wishes it or not the days of emotion will be over forever.

He is not ready. Not ready to face a future without passion, without hope. Without Clara. Not until he knows, for certain, that there is no way back to the love that had changed both their lives.

Later that day, as the barracks fall into darkness a lone vehicle leaves and heads for the city walls.

Ratzka prowls the hall swirling his robes behind him. The room is prepared for the ceremony, the women assembled in their finery all waiting with excitement to see the general remove his mask. Will the tales of his handsome face prove true? They know he has no woman now and wonders with jealous curiosity who will take the place of the red-haired beauty who had shared his bed for so many years. They all watch in silence as Ratzka paces back and forth like a caged beast, temper fraying more and more with every passing step. Finally, the strained rope that is containing his patience snaps.

"Where is he?" He hisses. "What kind of action is this. Does he have no respect?"

Marching to the door he summons a guard.

"Send men." Ratzka spits. "Bring General Aleric

to me now!"

Silence follows his words. In the hall no-one moves. They wait a long time until the guard returns.

"Well?" Ratzka is swiftly to his feet.

"I am sorry Governor the General cannot be found. He is gone."

"Gone!" The anger in Ratzka's voice strikes fear into the heart of the guard. "How can he be gone?"

"He has left the city. Alone. He was seen leaving in the hours of darkness."

"Find him." The words hang in the air like an executioner's blade. "Find him and bring him to me."

CHAPTER 36

Aleric drives slowly through the hills. The darkness that surrounded his exit has given way to dawn and now to daylight. He should reach the gap in the rocks by nightfall of the next day.

He knows that they will come looking for him, but they will be a full day behind him now. He has time but he has to be clever, he does not want to be found. This is something he must do for himself, alone. So, he twists and turns, taking side roads and driving over the bleached grass leaving a trail that will throw them off his scent, or at the least, slow them down. His heart beats swiftly and sweat pours down his neck onto his chest. He is tired but his adrenalin keeps him going. At last, when the heat of the day is past its highest and the clouds of dusk are starting to gather, he reaches the point where the track turns downhill. He looks up at the gap in the rocks, looking closely he can see the faint marks made by vehicles that have travelled through it.

His breathing slows, he cannot explain why but he knows that Clara is beyond those rocks. He has fought so hard to suppress his grief and loneliness and has tried to live the life that he had before she came but he knows it is impossible. Without her at his side, nothing is the same. All he craves is her presence in his bed, her body warm and soft beside him at night. He remembers the feeling of her holding him, staring into his eyes as he lay with her. Without her, he is not complete. He cannot begin to imagine a life without her in it and however long it takes he has to find her.

He imagines, inside his head, how their meeting will be. Will she run to him and press herself against him, relieved to be back in his arms? Or will the time away from him have brought doubts? Will her reunion with the brother he had been commanded to kill have changed her? He cannot allow himself to dwell on the latter. If she rejects him then he will go back and face his future; he has little doubt that he will be the one with a death sentence as desertion is unforgiveable. His failure to present himself to Ratzka will be seen as just that, desertion. But if she does reject him that is his only path, to face the council and hope for some degree of clemency; there is nothing he can be other than a soldier.

He turns towards the rocks, clinging to the hope that she is there, somewhere in the valley beyond and that she will welcome him and that their life together can start all over again.

Clara and Caval sit in the rear of Jarel's truck on some hessian sacks. The truck is jostling from side to side as it makes its way along the rough mountain tracks. She places her arm around the dog and steady's him as he tries to keep his balance,

She is nervous, edgy, and possessed by a restlessness she cannot explain. Caval senses it and whines constantly, pushing at her with his nose. The nerves had begun the day before this when she had been walking in the hills, following her recent liking of being alone where she could lose herself in memories, a sense of being watched, a feeling of someone being close to her that she could not shift. She shakes her head; she is being ridiculous. All that matters now is getting away from the convoy of vehicles that have been spotted; she knows who they are searching for, and they need to travel as far away from the village as possible. The truck grinds to a halt, the door swings open and Elle's head appears.

"Get out." She says sharply. "We are leaving the truck, it is too familiar, we go on foot to the next village. Jarel says we can hide there until we are sure they are gone, if we walk through the woods, they will not trace us."

Clara climbs out and beckons to Caval, attaching a piece of rope to his neck so that he will not run free and give them away, she starts to follow the others into the trees. As she walks, she feels it again, the sensation of someone being close to her. She spins and looks back into the open valley. On the far side, descending the mountain something is moving steadily downward. A single vehicle.

She catches her breath. She knows who follows them and her heart leaps as she whispers their name.

"Aleric."

Behind her the others are pushing on downwards, deeper, and deeper into the woods. Elle calls to her.

"Clara come on! We need to hurry."

Clara nods and begins to walk after them, but her feet feel heavy, and she moves slowly. Something is holding her back. Beside her Caval pulls backwards on the rope, disliking the restraint. She bends down and frees him. His tail wags and he looks up at her with his deep brown eyes. She smiles and takes the dog in her arms, love filling her veins. Her saviour, without him she would not have made her way through the past weeks. As she straightens something catches her eye, the vehicle has hit the plain and is making its way across the bleached grass. Shivers run down her skin and her throat tightens. The rest of her group are out of sight. Without knowing why, she does so she begins to walk towards the edge of the wood.

There she waits, a ragged, dirty figure with a

scruffy brown dog at her side, partly hidden by the trees, keeping herself in the shadows. One more look she tells herself, just one more then I will know for sure if my past life is truly behind me.

CHAPTER 37

The soldier climbs to the top of the hill and stops. He is breathing heavily. Before him, at the far side of the valley below is a deep wood that looks to go on for miles and miles. He is tired, they have been hunting the general for two days now and there has been no trace, he hopes that this will be the furthest point and that they can return to the barracks. Being out here, knowing that the rebels who brought the city to its knees surround them makes him nervous. Between himself and the wood is an open plain. He narrows his eyes and raises his glasses to them, scanning the empty space. Something in it catches his eye, the faintest glimmer, a sparkle of light alone in the barren ground. Retracing his steps he gets into his vehicle and calls the rest of the troop forward.

In the middle of the plain the sun is stronger and is at its peak. But the sweat that covers his body is not solely from the heat.

He raises his arm and summons his officer. He crouches low and his fingers reach for the object he has found, but he is afraid to touch it. The officer reaches him and stands beside him as slowly the soldier gets to his feet.

"What is it?" The officer halts beside him and the soldier hears the sharp intake of his breath.

They both stare at the object in silence.

Discarded, empty, glinting softly in the pale morning light is the golden mask of General Aleric.

THE END

I WOULD LIKE
TO THANK-

The following for their help and support in creating this book.

Phillip Jones- My talented, articulate son whose skill far exceeds mine but who has alwaysencouraged me to write.

Kayleigh Evans- For the video calls, the Whats App chats and the constant support through the author journey.

Dan Parsons- For being the walking encyclopaedia of publishing that he is.

All at the YHLP Writing Group for being the most welcoming and warm group of people I have ever met.

Pamela and Geoffrey Iveson for their lifelong friendship and never ending support.

Kassy Wiseman for her proof reading skills.

My dogs Covi and Romany for being company during the endless lonely hours that producing a book entails.

ABOUT THE AUTHOR

A.j.morris

A J Morris lives in the Welsh Valleys with her two Romanian Rescue dogs and a retired racehorse. Alongside writing she is an avid fan of Formula One and all Equestrian sports. She enjoys travel, art and literature and sings  in a community choir raising money for charity. Follow her on Instagram and Tik Tok : ajmorris_storyteller

BOOKS BY THIS AUTHOR

Winners

In 1934 a horse called Golden Miller achieved what has since seemed impossible; winning the Cheltenham Gold Cup and the Grand National in the same year. Since then many have tried to achieve the double and, so far, all have failed.

But when Tom Chichester comes across a horse called Olympic Run a dream takes shape that could change history. Struggling to keep afloat in a fiercely competitive world Tom is looking for the one horse that can make or break his career. Aided by his Kiwi jockey Rick and his team of hardworking staff Tom fights to not only succeed in his sport but overcome the threat of his jealous and embittered brother. Failed relationships, an unconventional love affair, disheartened owners and his own family set hurdles in his path at every turn.

Set in the often hard and heartbreaking world of jump racing Winners follows the fortunes and failures of Tom and his team through a season of racing as they aim to make history with their great hope Olympic Run

First

Meet Declan Hyde the star of the Matros Formula One team.

Talented and temperamental Declan's lifestyle is as fast as the cars that he drives. The arrival of a talented young "rookie" to the team threatens to disturb the status quo within the team he has helped create and remove his status as the team number one.

Then a meeting with an obsessed young fan sets off a chain of events that has catastrophic consequences..

First is a tale of love, rivalry, death and betrayal and follows Declan as his life changes and he faces the lowest point of his career.

Will he survive and regain his place at the head of the grid?

Travels With A Rescue Dog

One woman One Dog. One Holiday. What can possible go wrong?

Travels with a Rescue Dog is the true story of my holiday with my rescue dog. It is a non profit book being sold to raise money for The Dogs Trust

Printed in Dunstable, United Kingdom